Take the **A** Train

Also by Michael Blankfort

I Didn't Know I Would Live So Long
Behold the Fire
Goodbye, I Guess
The Strong Hand
The Juggler
The Widow Makers
A Time to Live
The Brave and the Blind
I Met a Man

The Big Yankee: The Life of
Gen. Evans F. Carlson

Take the A Train

MICHAEL BLANKFORT

HR

A Henry Robbins Book

E. P. DUTTON | NEW YORK

For information contact:
E. P. Dutton, 2 Park Avenue,
New York, N.Y. 10016

Library of Congress Cataloging in Publication Data
Blankfort, Michael, 1907–   Take the Ⓐ train.
"A Henry Robbins book."   I. Title.
PZ3.B6108Tak [PS3503.L477] 813'.5'2 78-1434
ISBN: 0-525-21360-0
Published simultaneously in Canada by Clarke, Irwin &
Company Limited, Toronto and Vancouver
Designed by Ann Gold

10 9 8 7 6 5 4 3 2 1

First Edition

For Sarah Blankfort Clothier,
the youngest of the tribe,
"so fair to look upon . . ."

Note to the Reader

In works of fiction the claim is often made that the characters are not based on people living or dead. This is a method of avoiding libel suits. I have always felt, however, that the disclaimer contains large elements of fraud. What novelist worth reading hasn't composed his characters from people, living or dead, whom he has known even casually? Writers fuel themselves by the intricate processes of imagination, but the life outside must be there as the bud to the flower. The inhabitants of this novel lived two lives—one in the world of their own time and another in the world that flourished in my head. Without the help of my many friends, black and white, of my old Harlem days, I could not have written this book. Of course, none is responsible for its contents.

I want also to acknowledge with gratitude and affection the encouragement of my friend Jane Pasanen.

Take the $\boxed{\text{A}}$ Train

1 Up to the day I tried to cheat Mr. Franklin Gilboa, my life seemed like something floating right out the window. I was going on seventeen—it seemed forever getting there what with school, summer camps, and trying to get along with the family, including my lousy older sister Marcy—and when I finally met Mr. Gilboa, not just to say hello and I'll be seein' ya, but the real thing, everything I was before then disappeared like spit on a hot griddle.

He ran the Sunset Arcade, a store filled with pinball machines on the boardwalk in Beachport, Long Island, and during that summer of 1947 I lost a fortune in nickels and dimes. The tall black man with his great sportshirts closed down the arcade when school started in September, and I figured I had to get even with him before then. One night when he wasn't looking I copied down the name of the company that made the machines and wrote them a letter saying I was going to open a place and would they send me the details on how much it would cost for three machines and what kind of take I could get. I typed the letter on a piece of paper I swiped from the fellow who ran a boathouse on Long Island Sound and put my address on it.

A week or so later I got back a hand-scribbled letter saying how much the machines would rent for and telling me I could figure out by myself how much the take should be by fixing a couple of headscrews in the base of the table. They even sent me a kind of blueprint, which I studied until I knew it by heart. I calculated how much the screws could be loosened to tilt the board so the balls would fall into the high-numbered holes. That way I could win enough chits for a Ted Williams bat or a Stan Musial glove, then sell them for some hard cash. I'd make up for the summer's losses and maybe come out ahead.

Now I didn't do all this planning to gyp Mr. Gilboa without feeling a little rotten about it. In the first place, I liked him for a lot of reasons, mostly because he didn't treat us like kids and always paid off what we won, and second, I thought he liked me more than anyone else in the gang even though we once had an argument which I won, kind of. But I never did anything you could call illegal before, if illegal is cheating a man whose pinball machines I was sure were fixed. Not to say that I was exactly Jack Armstrong the All-American Boy.

But I guess I was influenced by what I would hear at the house from Pop when he talked about his father, who was a tailor from the old country with a reputation for having, as he said, "a good name." Pop would tell me stories about how Grandpa had a chance to make lots of money under the table during World War I—and didn't. "He taught me," Pop said, "better to have little than live on stolen bread." Pop himself was an insurance salesman whose biggest fling was to go to the races and bet two bucks on a horse to show. His business, he told me, was an honest service to people. He never lectured to me and I liked him. Mom was different. I was scared of her. She ran the family like Top Sergeant Victor McLaglen. She was important in the neighborhood too, being vice-chairman of the Woodrow Wilson Democratic Party Club. There was a picture of her shaking hands with FDR in the dining room, and one of Mayor LaGuardia in the bedroom.

Of course, I hated doing something that would hurt my folks. But, after all, when certain people in your own family think you'll never amount to anything, you say the hell with it!

I never had any doubts that I'd make it work. As a matter of fact, my lousy sister Marcy called me Mr. Know-It-All, and I told her she was right. For as long as I can remember I had a real solid feeling that I knew more than the other kids about how to get what I wanted.

This didn't mean I wasn't careful. As much as I liked Mr. Gilboa, I was kind of scared of him too. Not because he was a black, the only *schwartzer* around Beachport. He didn't act tough and he didn't look it. He was tall, maybe over 6'2", and dressed like he just came out of an Ohrbach's or Abraham & Straus window. He had the voice of a doctor who wants you to believe it won't hurt just before he sticks the needle in your ass. Low and sure. And, boy, was he handsome. A chocolate-colored Gary Cooper. And black eyes as big as the wheels on a baby scooter. He laughed a lot, and though he was thin he looked as if he had just had a hell of a good meal. Satisfied, if you know what I mean. And then he had this way of putting a little air between him and the others so you'd never think of calling him Frank or Frankie. (Even when some of Mr. Gilboa's friends came over from Harlem to talk business, they called him Franklin.) He'd been in the war—I heard him say so once when an American Legionnaire came around for a donation—and he must've killed a lot of Nazis. The way I see it, once you get used to killing people, it isn't such a big deal.

The night before he closed was my D-Day. I figured I'd

get to my table early as usual, and when all the other kids came in I'd yell that I was feeling sick and ask him for a glass of water. He'd have to go to the crapper in the back, and I'd duck under the machine and loosen up the screws. I'd drink the water, of course, and thank him, saying I was feeling better, then begin to play.

You might ask why I didn't ask Eddie Norris, my best friend, to help me and divvy the prizes. Because Eddie was a *schmuck* and wanted someday to go before a court of law and swear he never did a crooked thing in his life. He's so square he even was bar-mitzvahed.

I was practicing with the balls—Franklin let us have a few warmups—and when the kids came in with their hot nickels and dimes and Franklin said okay fellows let's play, it's the last night, I yelled, "Hey, Mr. Gilboa, I ain't feeling so hot."

He came over quickly. "What's wrong?"

"I don't know. Maybe a glass of water. . . ."

He looked worried and went in the back. I ducked under the machine, found the screws in an instant, and loosened them easily. But I didn't count on Eddie. When he saw me drop to the floor, he ran over to me like a goddamn Red Cross nurse, yelling, "Help! Help!"

"Get outta here, you *schmuck!*" I whispered.

"What's the matter?" He was still yelling.

"Beat it!"

I kicked at him but he became more frightened and started pulling me out. Suddenly I saw Mr. Gilboa's face and a tan hand reaching for me. I don't know whether he saw the loosened screws, but I got to my feet, drank the water quickly, and said thanks, I feel better, I think I can play now.

"No, kid," he said. "Don't want to take a chance. You better sit down and rest a while."

"I'm okay," I yelled.

4

"Got a responsibility to your folks." He pushed me toward a broken chair in the corner and I saw Sam Schwartz, a real *schtunk*, move to my table. "Hey! That's mine. You can't play it!"

I begged Mr. Gilboa to tell that snotnose character to stay away from the machine.

"Why, kid?"

"I got a lot of dough invested in it."

"They're all alike, you know that."

"I'm used to that one!"

He turned to give someone change and I tried to move out of his hand. But he held on to me like a goddamn cop. My heart beat hard and black things crossed my eyes. His big eyes on mine made me dizzy. He laid a couple of fingers against the side of my neck and I figured he was on to me.

"Your heart's going too fast," he said. "That's healthy only when you're clumping a chick. No play for a while." He shoved me back into the chair.

"I'm okay, Mr. Gilboa."

"Not until I say so."

"That's the way my heart is sometimes." Which was a lie of course, because I never ever heard my heart before.

"You'd better go to a doctor."

"My heart's okay. Let me play my table."

He thought a minute, giving me a look that seemed to be counting the knots on my spine. "You got a hunch about the table, huh?"

"Yes, sir."

"Suppose you pick a friend to play it."

That was it. A lousy break. And I could see that I was up the creek. The guys were hanging around with big fish eyes, listening and watching. I hated them all. Not one had my guts. I was sore at myself too. How'd I let it go wrong? Eddie, that *schmuck;* if it wasn't for him.

5

"Let Eddie play my table," I said.

Eddie smiled like he had inherited my stamp collection, which I haven't looked at since I was six.

So I had to sit on that rotten chair and watch Eddie put his nickels in and yell like a taxidriver in a smashup every time he got the ball in a high number. I'd tell him someday that he was an accessory after the fact, an idea I picked up from a Brian Donlevy movie.

Now and then I got off the chair and went over to watch, feeling real sick as Eddie piled up the points and collected his chits. I'd look over to Mr. Gilboa, trying to show on my face that I was as healthy as Joe Louis, but he never even looked back.

When Mr. Gilboa called it a night, Eddie had won five packs of Camels, two lamps with Mickey Mouse shades, and a couple of penny ashtrays made of tin. What could you expect, I thought, from a kid who let his folks talk him into being bar-mitzvahed?

"Feeling okay?" Mr. Gilboa asked me as the kids started piling out of the door with their prizes.

"I told you I was," I said.

"Stick around, I want to talk to you."

Was he on to me? He'd never asked anyone to stay before. I watched him as he turned out the lights one by one, the store getting darker and I getting scareder.

"What time do you have to be home?" His voice came out of the dark.

"Any time," I said, trying to sound cocky.

"I don't want your Pop walloping you."

"He never does." I was proud saying that, not because Pop didn't dare but because he wasn't that kind of father. Besides, Mom did all the walloping in my family.

We walked out to the street. Most of the kids had gone home, except for Eddie, who was waiting for me under a lamp with a million bugs flying around it. It was a warm night, steam rising from the Sound a few blocks away. You could hear a tugboat and a whistle from some rich guy's cabin cruiser backing out of its slip.

I told Eddie to beat it, I was having a talk with Mr. Gilboa. I really wanted to ask him to follow me to make sure I was okay. But Eddie, his hands full of the *dreck,* turned up the boardwalk toward Prosser.

"If you see my folks," I called after him, "tell 'em I'll be home in a little while." That would tie me up with Mr. Gilboa if anything happened to me. You learn a lot from radio and movies.

We went in the opposite direction toward Miller Drive, where the big apartments were. We walked without saying anything past Honey's Beauty Parlor with the funny helmets in the window and a picture of a slick dame with a dress that didn't hide a thing. The corner Rexall was open but I couldn't see customers as we went by. I said "Hi" to Tony, who sold papers. Mr. Gilboa bought a *Daily News* and *Racing Form.* Another clue that might come in handy if I had trouble.

I grew up in this neighborhood. I knew every store and crack in the pavements, felt more at home there than in my own house; but during that walk with the tall thin man beside me, with neither of us saying a word, I felt like a stranger, like I'd never been there before. There was very little traffic, and the sound of our shoes on the sidewalk reminded me of one of those mystery movies. I wanted to say something about the heat of the baseball race, but my throat was dry. Besides, I wasn't a Dodger fan and that wasn't very popular in the neighborhood.

We slowed down at the corner of Mulvey and Webster, where the big red-bricked apartment house called Solomon's Arms began. I used to play handball against that wall and I'd get chased away by the tenants on the ground floor, a rabbi and his wife, who spoke terrible English. (My father once caught me yelling back, and he told me I mustn't because they'd been in a Nazi camp and had lost their children. That's when I stopped using their wall.)

"I live here," Franklin said.

I couldn't believe him. No *schwartzers* lived in any house in Beachport, and this one was all Jewish. Like where I lived. He led me through a side door where the garbage cans were, then down a flight of stone steps into the basement. A single bulb hung from the ceiling. We came to a heavy wooden door. He took out his keys, opened two locks, reached inside the door, and switched on some lights. He told me to go in and closed the door behind me, locking it.

"Want a coke?" he asked.

I nodded.

It was a big room, bigger than any in my folks' apartment. There were a lot of books all around, on chairs and on the floor and in wooden grocery cases. Piles of the *Racing Form* and other newspapers filled one corner. On the walls were large-sized pictures of women, mostly naked. I noticed that a lot of them were white, but some were black too. I hoped I'd have a chance to look at them closer, because I had only seen my sister naked and these looked different to me. I didn't notice the bed until later, but I did see a big Emerson radio and recordplayer and stacks of platters. A blackboard with numbers on it hung from a pipe on the ceiling. There were many pipes on the ceiling, fat and thin ones. It was hot in the room and I was sweating.

He brought me a coke and told me to sit down on a wooden kitchen chair next to a table. He sat on an easy chair made, I thought, of blue velvet or something like that. There was a strong lamp next to it and I could only see part of his face because of the shadows.

8

"The kids call you Doc," he said. "Why?"

"I don't know. . . ."

"What's your real name?"

"Henshel."

"Henshel what?"

"That's my last name. I hate my first name."

"What is it?"

"Melvin."

"I don't think it's bad."

What the hell did he know with a name like Franklin?

"Is your father a doctor?"

"No. . . ."

"What does he do?"

"Works. . . ."

"At what, kid?"

"Sells insurance."

He reached over and turned the recordplayer on, moving the volume to low. It was some good jazz. He said it was Count Basie. Then he picked up a small tin box and took out a reefer, lit it, and sucked the smoke in for so long I thought he'd never breathe again. He didn't pass it to me when he exhaled and I was glad because I had tried a stick once and coughed for a week.

"Maybe because you're a smart-ass," he said.

I was shaken by that and I didn't know how to answer.

"Maybe that's why they call you Doc."

I sipped the coke and tried to smile at the same time. It didn't work and I got some of the coke up my nose.

"I've been watching you, Doc. For two summers now. . . ." He took another deep drag. Then, letting out the smoke in little spurts, he reminded me of the time a year ago when we had a hassle about his not letting us carry over our chits from one day to another. He wouldn't go for it. "It's lousy business," he had said. "Got to be fair to myself too. Finish the day. Finish the play. Can't count on tomorrow. You don't want to play, don't play." I remembered how angry I was. Ashamed of losing the battle. I was sure I was right but that didn't help me. The kids were waiting around for me to do something. I could still see Mr. Gilboa's eyes. Not angry exactly. Not giving in either. There was something else there that time. Like we were both grown-ups together and he was testing me to see how far I'd go. I felt a kind of charge, like betting on a horse to win against long odds. Like standing on a high diving board with my guts choking me and knowing I had to jump. Then I heard myself say, "Okay, Mr. Gilboa, we'll take your deal. But you give us four balls for a nickel instead of three." And, by God, he agreed!

He was smiling now. "Ever since that night, I had an eye on you, Doc. A smart-ass kid who had the guts to be smart."

I wanted to say something and I didn't know what, but this time it didn't matter. I liked the way he was nodding and grinning. He asked me what I wanted to do when I grew up. I said I didn't know. He said to think about it. I thought: My father wanted to be a doctor but he sold insurance. My Uncle Jack wanted to be a musician but he was selling women's dresses. My sister Marcy wanted to transfer to Vassar or Radcliffe but she couldn't go unless she had a scholarship.

"I want to make lots of money," I said.

"Good. But the question is—what for?"

"To put in a bank."

"Hell, man, money's for spending. Not for saving. Don't give it a chance to curdle in your pocket. Lay it out, give it away, stir it around on chicks, nags, cars, clothes. Make every buck a holiday buck. Hey, ever see a Brinks truck follow a hearse?" He waved a long arm to take in his apartment. "Don't let this palace fool you, boy. This is summertime and I lazy myself here where the heat ain't so bad and the money ain't bad either. And there's always something coming in on the side. And more when certain things get settled. Which they're about to do. So don't go crying 'savings' around me. It's an absolutely inhuman word made up for suckers by banks and insurance companies."

He lay back in his chair, smoking while I finished the coke. I liked the things he said.

"Ever hear of capitalism, Doc? You did. Saw it in the papers, huh? Well, I'm for it. And you know why? Because it means that people got to spend their bread fast. And that's good for me and my business. Ever it slows up, this spending, we slide right into a depression. Which is what my old man preached in Baltimore, Maryland. Way back in the thirties, but no one listened to him." He laughed. "Man, you got a lot to learn. How you going to make all that money?"

"I don't know. . . ."

"Legit? You want to make it legit?"

I didn't say anything, not knowing the answer.

He turned the record over. "Let me tell you something, Doc. There's legit and there's legit. Take my pinball machines. You think they're fixed. Just the odds, that's all. In my favor. Over a summer I know almost to the penny how much I'm going to make. Nothing wrong with playing with the odds, is there? No. Okay. It's within the law. Now, there are other things I do that's not within the law, but that don't make it dishonest. Take horseracing. Bet at the track, okay. Bet on the street, the cops'll get you if you don't pay 'em off. But there's no cheatin'. Just the odds. Now, you can be crooked in a legal business and you can be honest in an illegal business. Are you listening, boy? You're looking at me, but I can't tell if you're listening. Okay. I'm an honest gambler. I pay what I owe to the penny and to the minute. And the rest of the world downtown in the stores and Wall

Street houses and banks, that's another business. Mostly shit, I think. But I get mine and they get theirs, and they're not any better than I am. Okay?"

I said okay. I was taking in every word he said, though I wondered why he was saying all that to me. He leaned forward and lit the reefer, which had gone out, but he let it burn without smoking.

"Being honest doesn't mean being smart," he went on with a sudden grin showing large white teeth. "I can use a smart-ass like you, and a white one's something special." He thought for a moment, rubbing the side of the velvet chair. "These days anyway. Kind of a passport. Gets you up to places a nigger can't go yet."

I felt like I'd been given a medal for winning the hundred-yard dash at the Police Athletic Club games.

"But, as I say, being smart sure don't mean being honest either."

What was he telling me? I began to sweat again, and my heart beat so loud I thought he could hear it.

"A friend of mine cheats on me, no matter who—my brother, my son, even my father—he's through, wiped out." He raised his arms toward me as if to pull me to him. "You see these broken thumbs?"

I nodded quickly. I could see that they stuck out from his hand at an angle and had big knobs on them.

"I got them in a gang fight over on Lenox and 141st when I was twelve. They were broken when I wouldn't tell on a friend. That's loyalty. That's honesty. That's legit. I respect trust and loyalty in a man or he ain't worth the crap on a sheet of pink toilet paper." He lowered his hands, lit the reefer again, and pulled in a lungful of smoke.

"You ever been laid, boy?"

I hated to say so but I told him no.

"How old are you?"

"Seventeen—soon."

"Shee-it, you're wasting away. And you're big for your age. Time, boy. That's all we got. Time and a lot of ever-new gism. Know what I mean? You do? Good. See all those pretties on the wall? I laid every one of 'em. I started when I was ten, and there's a lot more chicks in the world just waiting."

Suddenly I had this idea. With Franklin Gilboa I would find the right way to show what I could do in life. He was Spencer Tracy, Humphrey Bogart, and Brian Donlevy all in one package. He was Super Pop. I wanted him to like me, to trust me.

"I got something to tell you, Mr. Gilboa."

"You have, eh?" He rubbed the top of his shiny smooth black hair and eased back in his chair.

"I—I tried to cheat you. . . ."

"You did, did you?"

I couldn't tell whether he was angry or not because I couldn't look at him straight.

"I fixed the machine. . . ."

"Now how did you do that?"

"I learned about the set screws underneath. . . . I got the word from the company that makes the tables."

"Is that when you said you were sick?"

"Yes, sir."

He hummed a little, closed his eyes for a moment, and laid down the stick. "Why did you tell me now?"

"Because. . . ."

"Come on." It was a command.

"I want you to trust me."

"And what else do you want?"

"I want to be like you."

He stood up, laughing and slapping his hands together as if he were going to dance to the music from the record-

13

player. "Want to be like me! Oh, lady, lady! It ain't like fallin' outta bed." He was smiling and laughing and I thought he'd never stop. "Want to be like me, eh?"

"Yes, sir."

He stopped laughing and sat down again. "Get it outta your head, kid. You ain't gonna be like me. Not in a million years. You startin' out with the wrong color. And you gotta learn early how to eat shit. Then work into your gut the rules of the game they play by, and when you're done with that you stick your little finger into a crack somewhere, then a hand, an arm, and you finally push your way through until you make your own shit and let others eat it. So, white boy, I like you and all that, but you ain't ever gonna be Franklin Gilboa, never!" He smiled suddenly. "Hell, don't feel bad. There ain't a nigger in Harlem can be just like Franklin Gilboa!"

He took a long deep breath and wiped his hands together like he had won a big bet.

"You're finished cheatin' on me?"

"Yes, sir, Mr. Gilboa."

It was hard looking up at him, he was so tall. But I wanted him to see that I meant it.

"What do you think, boy? Was I on to you or not?"

"You were on to me," I said, shaking all over.

He sat down on the velvet chair. "Never going to cheat again? Nobody!"

"No, sir."

"Got good feelings now?"

"Yes, sir."

"Unless you got good feelin's," he said, "you oughta be put away for trespassin'. Christ should've done all the sufferin' for us but the communications got mixed up. Like they did in the Battle of the Bulge. . . . Your folks religious, boy?"

14

"They're Jews," I said.

"I know that!"

"Well, what's religious?"

"Do they go to temple? Do they eat pork? Do they teach ya an honest deal is the only deal?"

"They do, but—look, I don't know about religion. Sometimes they go to temple and sometimes they don't. But they didn't care when I said I didn't want to get bar-mitzvahed like Eddie Norris. They collect money sometimes for Palestine Jews. Mom's a regular politician. In more clubs than you can count. She runs around to get votes on Election Day and comes near to living at the Democratic Party office on Webster Street. She's a member of the NAACP."

He laughed a little. "I know the type. Loves Mrs. Roosevelt, Henry Wallace, and—"

"She's got pictures of FDR and LaGuardia all over the house. Signed."

"I got me a son too. . . ."

"What?"

"I said I got me a son."

I felt a little dizzy. I never thought of his being married.

"Name's Brian. Lives with his mother in Florida. Your age."

I tried to be polite. "That's nice." But I didn't mean it and I wasn't sure why.

"I haven't seen him much," he said. "Not for a long time. A helluva long time. Gets into trouble down there too. His mama keeps him away from me."

"I'm sorry. . . ."

"You see any tears in my eyes, boy, forget it. It's only dirt from the air."

I knew he was putting it on.

"I sure wish it was different," he said. "But wishin' is like pissin' against the wind." He sighed, took in a deep swing of the reefer, kept it down, and let it out like smoke signals. He closed his eyes, then opened them on me like he was surprised that I was there. "He don't think half as much of me as you do."

I felt sorry and good at the same time.

"My son's your age. Right to the year, from what you told me. But bein' born don't give you squatter's rights, does it?"

"No, sir."

"Your folks'd be real sore if they knew you were hangin' around a reefer-smokin' numbers man."

"My Pop goes to the races."

"That's no answer."

"Yeah, they'd be sore."

He scratched the back of his neck. Later on I would see him do the same thing at the track when he was making up his mind about a horse.

"We'll hold off for a while tellin' 'em," he said.

"Okay." More than okay.

He kept studying me, and I'll be damned if his eyes weren't teary.

"Got a bookful to teach a young fellow. And I don't mean about numbers, whores, and horses. I mean about human-ology. Know what that is? You don't, huh? Well, give us time, you'll know." He squinted at me through the smoke. "You happy, boy?"

I never thought about using a word like that, but I said what came right into my mind. "No."

"Why not?"

"I don't know."

"Don't get on with the folks?"

"I don't know."

"Got brothers and sisters?"

"One sister. Marcy. She's at City College."

He kept at me, saying that he could read people right and

he'd read me. I had something worming in the belly, something biting bitter and growing. "Not that you got a wood-chip on the old shoulder, boy, but I can read that you want to show off how spit-bright you are. Like when you talked me into givin' you the four balls 'stead of three. You were doin' that not just for the extra chance or bigger score but to come out on top of me and the kids in your gang. Fightin' to prove you got somethin' nobody else has."

He smoked the reefer, staring at me, and I began to think he could see right through my skin. It scared me. I hated what was happening with my eyes and mouth. I had a ball in my throat and I couldn't swallow it or spit it out.

Suddenly I heard myself cry out, "They don't think I'm worth a shit."

"Who's they?"

"Pop and Mom."

"Why?"

"I don't know."

"You know, boy. Don't try to plead me off."

"I don't know!" I yelled.

He let it go and didn't say anything for a while. The smoke from the pot got around to me and I breathed it in. The clock was ticking louder, and when he moved the spring in his chair made a racket. I felt sick because I knew there was something wrong in talking about Marcy and the folks. Like being a traitor.

"I saw that in you," he said. "Hating to go home when the joint closed up. Looking for showoff space. Could mean trouble, boy, if someone doesn't keep an eye on you. I thought to myself: There's a good kid with a brain. I went out to you like I remembered myself way back when—I said to myself there's a kid that's just startin'. Can go either way. I could use him for my sake. Ain't goin' to be in policy all my life. A white brain, real sharp. I got vibrations about you.

Saved my life in the war a couple of times feelin' vibrations. What to do, what not to do, when to move, when to keep the old head down. That get to you, Doc? You understand?"

"Yes, sir."

I could see he was giving me the eye again, his big black ones reading right through me.

He looked at his watch. It shone in the light, gold with diamonds and rubies on the case.

"Hell, it's after twelve. Better beat it home before LaGuardia comes down off that wall!"

We walked to the door and out came his keys.

"Tomorrow," he said, "come by Rossini's Barbershop on Market Way. In the afternoon after school."

"Okay, Mr. Gilboa."

The door was opened.

"Good night, Doc."

"Good night, Mr. Gilboa."

"Call me Franklin, boy."

I couldn't see his face in the shadows, but I knew I had won the big prize after all. We were going to be friends.

I ran through the empty streets toward my house like Ralph Kiner after he hit four home runs in two games back to back. I wasn't really going home. What I felt was that I was leaving my home and going to spend the night with a couple of second cousins called Pop and Mom.

2 Well, you could guess who was waiting up for me when I turned the key into the front door of the apartment—Detective Sergeant Mom and Beat Cop Pop. And they weren't looking chummy, even in their bathrobes. On their faces was this funny look that was halfway between "We know you'll lie" and "We must show we believe you because that's the way to bring up children these days."

"It's after twelve," Pop said, his voice like an iceberg.

"My watch stopped."

"You're supposed to be in by eleven."

After D-Day I got them to push the deadline from ten to eleven on no-school nights.

"Let's see your watch," Mom said.

"I fixed it when I saw the clock in Kramer's window."

"Where were you?" Pop asked.

There's a rule that says the whole truth and nothing but the truth. But I learned it can't work with parents. I don't know why. The law's on their side—the law of pocket money, clothes, food, a place to sleep—and the law doesn't figure the way we do. It comes down to the fact that parents can't handle the truth, that's all. It's too much for them.

Mom was a regular lady district attorney with a weight problem. (Pop had given up throwing his own weight around, which kept him thin.) They weren't anything like Franklin. I mean, like I knew already that Franklin wasn't going to treat me like a kid who owes him something and has to keep up with the payments.

"So your father asked you a question. Where were you?"

The best lie is a kind of truth, so I said I was talking with the man who ran the pinball arcade because it was closing night and he wanted me to stay around and help him. Mom asked his name, which was easy, and then she asked what we talked about.

"Nothing much," I said and started for the bedroom.

"Sit down," Mom said. "We're talking to you."

"I gotta go to the toilet."

"Marcy's in there. You'll have to wait," Pop said.

That didn't surprise me because she was always in the can, reading her wacky books.

I sat down but they didn't get much more out of me. I had to listen to Mom say that Pop was worried, as if I didn't know that she was the one who always kept track of things. Like she was the chief dispatcher at Penn Station. If she didn't know everything, Pop and Marcy and me'd collide every hour on the hour.

"Saul, you know this man he's talking about?" she asked Pop.

He said he'd seen him around, a *schwartzer* who had a shoeshine stand on Market Way and ran the arcade at the beach. Mom always said she liked people no matter what their color or religion, so she couldn't object to his being colored. She backed away into blaming me for forgetting that tomorrow was the first day of school and why didn't I want to be with them instead of staying out so late when I needed sleep to get ready, and next time to be home at eleven or else things would happen I wouldn't like.

I didn't bother to look at Pop, who was cleaning his glasses with a dollar bill, because he didn't ever try to tackle Mom. He let her walk away with everything without a fight. I said good night as polite as I could and went into the kitchen to pick up some leftovers in the fridge. I get hungry when I'm excited, and I was still high from Franklin. Since it was Sunday night and we'd had deli for supper, I found some tongue slices and Mom's homemade cole slaw—which is the best thing she ever made—and also a large slice of apple pie and some Swiss cheese. I didn't know how excited I really was.

Marcy and I shared the same can and, as I guessed, she was still in it as usual when I left the kitchen.

"Hey, Marcy," I called and knocked on the door. "Finish up, will you?"

"I'm washing my hair."

Washing her hair! That's all she ever did because she had long blonde hair and she didn't want it to get dark with dirt. Me, I got coal-black hair, but who gives a damn what color it looks? Besides I didn't hear the water going and I figured she was just being her lousy self. I told her I had to go to the can and she said she was doing her best. I kicked the door a couple of times and said I knew she wasn't washing her hair and if she didn't get the hell out right away I'd go into her bedroom and pee all over her floor. She knew I wouldn't do it and she called me a boor, a bum, an animal, but she unlocked the door between my bedroom and the can. The place stank with her shampoo, and books were all around— on the floor, the washbasin, the top of the crapper, and the laundry basket. She was a reader, that Marcy; it was a goddamn disease and she gobbled up the stuff like a kid with unlimited credit at Goldberg's Drugstore. She never read one book at a time, and how she kept track I'll never know.

As I said, she was at City College but hoping, if Pop had the money or she got a scholarship, to transfer to some highbrow girls' college up in New England. And how my folks ate it up. Christ, you'd think knowing the difference between Keats and Shelley or between Jefferson and Hamilton was positively religious—I mean, like believing in God and fasting on Yom Kippur. But, as I said, the folks drove me crazy boasting to everybody about Marcy, her straight A's, her high IQ and State Regents scores.

And that wasn't all. The word got around. I'll never forget when I was a freshman at Beachport High. Marcy was a senior then. It was in my American history class, which I liked, but not Mr. Traugott, who taught it. A real sourpuss who liked to throw curves at the kids. He'd make fun of the slow ones, correct mistakes as if he got his kicks out of them, and slash our exam papers with all kinds of rotten remarks like "Lincoln may have freed the slaves but he forgot you!" Or "The reasons you give for the opening of the West might have kept it closed forever!"

On one test my paper came back with no mark on it, just a scrawl: "You ought to do better!" I raised my hand, and when he called on me I asked him what mark he had given me and where I had made mistakes. He walked down the aisle toward me.

"Sketchy," he said. "Not complete enough. You're not thinking, Henshel."

I said something under my breath like "Shit, that don't help."

He heard me and said so everyone could hear, "I had your sister in my class three years ago. She never did a paper as bad as yours. Can't you keep up?"

I don't know what happened next. I blinded, hauled off and socked him. The next thing I knew I was down in the principal's office getting hell for hitting a teacher. I told him I didn't care, he had no right to say what he did. He kept me there until Mom arrived. And right in front of everybody she took their side, and when we got home she made a big speech about how I could be as good as Marcy if I only paid more attention.

That did it for me. I wasn't going to run a race with Marcy my whole life. That was one I couldn't win. So I started pissing the time away, fooling around with the kids in the streets and with the boatyard workers instead of doing homework, copying Eddie Norris', lying like crazy to the folks. And after cheating on the exams in all my subjects, I got a 65 average, enough to get promoted.

I wouldn't be like Marcy if DiMaggio himself got down on his hands and knees and begged me.

That night after I met Franklin I got into bed and turned my radio on low. It was too late for "I Love a Mystery" so I tuned in the Cotton Club with Cab Calloway. What would Franklin want from me when I saw him tomorrow? Saying I was wasting my time being a virgin—did that mean he'd get me a dame?

Sam Schwartz, who hung around with me and Eddie Norris—a putzy kind of guy with a whine like a rubber doll but lots of ready cash for tennis balls, chocolate frosteds, dirty postcards, and tickets for the Polo Grounds (which his mother's boyfriend gave him)—boasted a lot about dames. And I didn't let him think he was ahead of me. I guess the truth is, as I said, that up to this time I was a junior Dick Tracy. In a way, that is. Sure, I'd fooled around with Marie Anderhorst, whose father was the super where we lived, and with Diana Levy, my first cousin who liked to mush around with me when her folks came to supper on Saturday nights. But that was nothing.

I figured I'd better get some sleep, stop thinking, you know, to save myself for the real thing. But I kept hearing Franklin asking me what I wanted to be when I grew up. The first thing I ever wanted to be, maybe when I was six or eight—and this'll kill you—was a rabbi. Yes, an honest-to-God rabbi like the one who came to see Pop when he was sick. I thought he was wonderful with his black beard, a voice like drums in an American Legion parade, and pockets full of raisins and almonds. I used to wait for him to come every day, standing behind the front door, to touch him as he walked by. He would stop, say "Good afternoon, young man," in that deep voice, and I'd stick my hands into his pockets until I'd taken out all I wanted. Mom never liked him. She was always in a hurry to get him out of the house and didn't ever ask him to have a cup of tea. Later I heard her and Pop make fun of him, and after a while I didn't think so much of him either.

In my mind I went through a lot of other things I wanted to do when I grew up, but even thinking about them gave me a pain in the belly.

The fact is I never did know what I wanted to be before I told Franklin. Now I knew. To be like him. I had this feeling that Franklin owed nothing to nobody. That he came and went whenever he wanted to. That he could stay out all night or eat when he was hungry, not when someone decided it was time to. That he was his own boss. That he didn't worry about rent or taxes, like my father and Uncle Jack did. That he had all the women he ever wanted and he didn't have to marry them or take any bullshit from them. That if any woman bossed him as Mom bossed Pop he'd throw her out on her ass. That he knew a helluva lot, I mean, about where things were and how to fix them if they need to be fixed. That he had fun! I mean, that if things weren't fun and good times, he'd just walk away from them. That he didn't care about what Marcy called "duty" or Mom called "responsibility." That he was strong, that he knew exactly where he wanted to be every minute of the day and night. That he was like Bill Holden, a cowboy in a picture I saw years before called *Texas*. He went from dancehall to dancehall having a helluva time, picking up enough dough when he needed it, driving cattle from Abilene to Kansas City if he felt like getting a looksee at a big city, and always, no matter what happened, on top of things. That was it—being on top of things! A guy who could booze it up and know, damn it, that he was better, stronger, smarter, faster in the head and on the draw than anyone around.

Now, as I've said from time to time, I was born with that kind of thing too. If I wanted, I could become a millionaire, a general in the Army, a doozie with the dames, top dog at anything. Marcy with all her books would have to work hard for what I was born with. And that's why, I guess, I took so quickly to Franklin—because I think he saw what I had, and I saw that he had the same thing.

The question was how to get out of the trap I was in. I mean, parents, going to college, becoming a lawyer, which my folks kept saying they expected me to be. Franklin Gilboa—he was the way out. The only way.

3 Next day as soon as I hiked through registration, marching from room to room in a line of kids like a screwy chain gang, I lied to Eddie Norris, who wanted me to come to his street afterward to play handball, and ran the long mile to Market Way and Rossini's Barbershop and Beauty Salon, where Franklin had a shoe stand in an alley next door. A bunch of people were around him—Mario from Kaplan's Liquor and Deli, Bobby from Rexall's, Mrs. Gumbracht from the checkout counter at the A&P, and Mrs. Anderhorst, Marie's fat mother. I used to pass the place a dozen times a week on my way to the beach, but I never noticed that so many people hung around the shoeshine stand without getting their shoes shined.

They were giving Franklin money and slips of paper. He waved me over to one side and asked me how it went last night when I got home.

"Okay," I said.

"Folks give you hell for staying out late?"

"Nope." He squinted his eyes like he had taken some castor oil and I said, "Not much."

"How was school?"

"Lousy."

He moved out of the sun, which had made his light brown skin seem almost blue, and touched his side pockets filled with slips. "You know what they're for?"

I told him I did.

"I want you to go to my place," he said, taking out a bunch of keys and slipping two of them off the ring. "Near the recordplayer is a pile of platters. Find 'Slow Boat to China.' Inside the jacket is an envelope. Bring it to me. And don't forget to lock up both locks when you leave."

Like in a Garfield or Bogart movie I ran from Market to Solomon's Arms and opened the side door the way I had seen Franklin do it. Inside, the room was dark and I turned up the lights. The place didn't seem as big as the night before. I went over to the Emerson recordplayer, noticing a big closet with the door open and a row of suits inside. Must have been thirty, forty. On the floor below were shoes to match. And each one with a polish you could light a room with. He sure didn't dress that way at the arcade or the barbershop. I took a quick gander at some of the pictures on the wall. Wow! What boobs! And legs! What I had seen in front of the Ritz Burlesque House was nothing! Absolutely nothing!

There was a lot to look at but, not wanting to take more time, I got out the thick envelope, turned off the lights, double-locked the door, and ran back to Franklin.

"How much did you bring me, boy?" he asked.

I was stumped. "How should I know?"

He smiled, his neat white teeth shining, and told me to take the envelope to an address near Penn Station in Manhattan. Then he gave me the fare up and back from Beachport and a five-dollar bill. "That's for you," he said.

I made the three-thirty train and I was on my way. The

stations went by fast as a merry-go-round. Oceanside, East Rockaway, Jamaica—the mick conductor calling them out half asleep—Kew Gardens, Forest Hills, Penn Station. I had to be careful there because my Uncle Jack had his showroom for ladies' dresses across the street. But being careful wasn't being afraid. I knew I'd get away with it because that's the way I was built.

It was easy to find the address on 33rd Street right off Seventh. A boarded-up store with a sign saying SHOE RE-PAIR. A colored fellow was standing a couple of feet away from the door talking to a cop. I thought I'd better wait, but the colored fellow saw me and nodded. The cop didn't even look at me and I went in.

The place was ratty and dark with the smell of old jock-straps and cigars. Some guys, white and black, were study-ing a blackboard with the race results, like they couldn't believe what they saw. Behind a kind of wooden counter a fat old dame was dozing with her eyes open. When I came in she gave me a quick look, then banked her head again on her thick shoulders.

"Hey, Doc!"

Christ, who knew me?

In the corner a black fellow with a mustache and gold-rimmed specs on the tip of his nose was waving to me. Next to him was a real dude with a wide black hat and a check-ered suit.

"You Doc, ain't ya?" the black man asked.

"Yeah."

"I'm Hayes. Friend of Franklin's. He give you somethin' for me."

"He didn't say anybody's name."

"It's okay, kid. He called. Said you was comin'."

"Yeah, but—"

"How'd I know your name was Doc if he didn't tell me?"

27

Well, that made sense, so I gave him the envelope. The dude's eyes were all over me. Hayes turned his back to us and opened the envelope. After a minute he gave it to the dude. "It's all there," he said. "You're a lucky roller, man."

"Y'all's the lucky one," the dude said.

"He hit a triple with a fiver," Hayes said to me. "Three grand."

The dude was still counting the money.

"It's all there, Billo," Hayes said.

"Stop interruptin'," the dude said.

"Want a coke or somethin'?" Hayes asked me, but I said I was okay and was there anything he wanted me to take back to Beachport. At that moment the phone rang. The fat old dame answered and yelled to Hayes that Franklin was on.

"The kid's here okay," Hayes said into the phone. "And the guy's paid off." He turned to me. "Franklin said for you to get back on the next train. He don't want you to have no trouble with your folks."

"Won't be no trouble," I said, hearing myself imitate him. I did a lot of that when I was with Franklin and his friends.

"Where you-all goin' to, kid?" the dude asked. He had a real Southern accent.

"Beachport, Long Island."

"You been a messenger of good luck, boy," the dude said, " 'cause if you didn't come when you did with the bread, there'd be a salty mess roun' here. Been laying five bucks on that number forevah, and goddamn it when it comes ridin' in I want the bread right warm in my hands. I hate waitin'. Hear that, Hayes?"

"I heard ya," Hayes said.

"Come on, kid," the dude said, "I'll drive ya home."

He had a red Buick that rode like a ball-bearing skate. He didn't speak much but kept looking over at me now and then. I was beginning to be sorry I hadn't taken the train.

28

Before we got to the 59th Street Bridge he said, "I got my place near here. Want to come up for a minute?"

"I gotta get back," I said.

"Won't be long, kid."

"Better not."

"Nothin' to worry about."

"It ain't that. . . . Gotta get home, that's all."

"How much bread you make today?"

"Five bucks."

"Five lousy bucks. Christ, you work for me, I'd give you more than that."

I thought: I wouldn't work for you for all the bullets shot in the war. "Look, sir, if you're in a hurry to do somethin', you don't have to take me home. I'll pick up the subway to Penn Station."

"No hurry. Jus' want to stop off for a couple of minutes. Got some groovy platters. You like Louie?"

I was sweating a little. His eyes were wetting up and his fingers moved against the steering wheel, up and down around the rim like it was too hot to hold. One time down at the beach a couple of fruits tried to pick up me and Eddie Norris. I figured that something had to be done soon, because if he touched me I'd have to find a way of kicking him in the balls. Sitting next to a guy in the front seat of a car doesn't make that easy.

"I'm a friend of Mr. Gilboa's," I said, thinking somehow that would stop him.

"So what?" He didn't sound stopped.

He turned onto First Avenue. What the hell, I could jump out at the next red light, but I hated to do that. It meant running away, and that was not for me. Besides, I figured I was smarter than the dude. So I began to work over the old think box.

"Got some high-class kif," the dude said.

I didn't know what kif was, but it didn't sound right.

"Get you some new clothes," he said, tapping his fingers on the wheel.

We came to a red light. I moved my hand toward the door, but I hated to show how scared I was.

The car reached 63rd Street and slowed down in front of a brownstone house.

"Here we are, sugar," the dude said.

The old think box came through. "I got crabs," I said.

He jerked the car to a stop and screamed, "You lousy little punk. Get the fuck outta the car!"

The next day Franklin asked me about the dude. "How'd it go?"

"Okay." I wasn't going to bring Franklin into my problems.

"He make a pass at you?"

"No. . . ."

"What the hell does that mean?"

"He didn't touch me."

"I didn't ask if he touched you. Did he make a pass?"

"He wanted me to go to his place."

"Yeah? So what happened?"

"I'm no queer. So I told him I had crabs. And he threw me out of the car. You don't have to worry about me!"

"The hell I don't. You're a kid, and a whitey at that, and I don't want anything to happen to you. I bawled the shit out of Hayes for letting you go with the dude. It works both ways, Doc. If you're my friend and work with me and I trust you, then I got duties too. To take care of you, that's my job. See that nothing happens to you. Nothing at all." He wiped his face. I saw that he was sweating. "Now I'll get you some ointment for the little fellows."

I'd fooled him too. I say things in a way that sells people. Like an actor.

"I was jazzin' the dude," I said, smiling.

"Kee-rist, Doc, you're slippery elm. And good as a preacher caught in a whorehouse. But you're never goin' to lie to me or I'll break your legs."

I didn't think I ever would, so it was easy to say I wouldn't.

Franklin asked me a couple of weeks later if I'd like to make some money after school hours, a real easy question. He gave me a job as a runner in a couple of streets in Oceanside, which was okay with me because no one there knew my folks. They were foreigners who worked for the Long Island Railroad—Polacks, Russkies, Italians, and Jews who were poorer than those living in my town. I brought money when they won and took their bets—6 to 1 on the first number of the total take of three races at certain tracks, 60 to 1 if they picked two numbers of the total, and 600 to 1 if they got the first three.

Women did the betting while their husbands were at work or looking for it. Even when I had bad news, they'd tell me to come in and have a coffee and some homemade cake. Also, I never heard such crazy ideas. "What's your name?" some dame would ask me, and when I told her she'd count the letters slowly and bet on thirteen. Or one and three. One nice lady who couldn't speak much English dumped her pocketbook upside down to let the change fall on the kitchen table. Then she closed her eyes and picked up a coin and bet the last number on the date. One Russian dame had a painting of a saint and talked to him, asking what number she should take. And others would tell me their dreams and explain why the dreams meant such and such a pair or triplet numbers.

I knew the odds, and it was crazy to bet. I figured it gave these dames something to think about other than work or kids or doing the washing. Maybe when they scored good, they'd have something on their husbands.

Franklin told me once that life was like having to kiss a thousand asses. "There's the Con Edison ass, the telephone ass, the landlord ass, the bread-butter-and-potato ass, the next-war ass, the cancer ass, the undertaker's ass. And gamblin' is a way you hope you'll get one big fat juicy ass to ease off all the other asses. That's why I'm in the rackets. It's one big round sugarsweet mama ass, and it sure handles a lot of little ones." He patted me on the head. "Every man got to find himself one, or he's a bum. Don't care what it is. You'll get yourself a legit ass sooner or later. I mean, having the smarts like you and being nice and white. That's what I want for you—real legit. But there's lots to learn, boy. Lots. . . ."

I didn't like bringing my customers bad news and taking their money for the next day's run, even if it was a penny, nickel, and dime business. But to the dames it was like going to church or having a tree at Christmas time. I could see that they got a jolt out of my coming by every afternoon, and if I didn't they'd be disappointed. The coffee and cakes were there, win or lose. Even the big wet kiss on the forehead, which, to come clean, I didn't care for. That is, except when I brought a winner. Then I got a real kick out of them, even the hugs.

I made some good friends with the women. Even the husbands, who I saw now and then when they were laid off, didn't worry when their wives got excited with the winnings I brought them and pushed my head right smack up to their boobs.

I bet a nickel a day across the board and never won. But more than anything I got the biggest kick going with Franklin across the river to Harlem. The streets hopped up and down with crowds of kids and grown-ups moving around, yelling, laughing, fighting. Smell of fried chicken and pork. Bars and fish-fry joints every couple of blocks with juke boxes rocking your ears when you passed by. Radios blasting from open windows, kids playing stickball, sewer covers as bases. And the chicks. Man, sometimes you'd see one coming toward you when you're walking with Franklin and she's got this shining green dress on her cocoa-colored skin, earrings floating from the sides of her head, and a pocketbook swinging like one of those pendulums on a grandfather clock. She comes up to Franklin and says, "H'ya, Mr. Gilboa. Who's the sugar boy with you?" Franklin'd say he's my friend Doc. She'd tell me I'd lucked out having him as my friend, and Franklin would give her butt a gentle little pat and you'd think he'd made her a present of his Caddie.

Everybody seemed to go for Franklin. I used to think it was because he was so handsome and wore clothes that were sharper than a dude's because he'd get them at one of the big downtown New York stores and not in Harlem. But I found out just by watching that it was more. Lots of guys and dames would come up to him, say their "H'ya Franklin" or "What ya doin', Mr. Gilboa?" and tell him some hard-luck stories. He'd listen as if he were a preacher, I mean, listen hard and careful, then hand out bread like a bakery.

He'd stop in to places to show me his hangouts: Small's and the Cotton Club; the Hotel Theresa at 125th and Seventh, filled with dudes, chicks, and sweating business fellows; Thelma's Bar, where the downtown white musicians got drunk even in the afternoon; and Eppie's, a restaurant where he went when he felt like niggerish food, as he put it—you know, greens, grits, fried yam, and pork. Eppie herself showed him his table and brought him the menu. You'd think he was Nat King Cole or General Marshall or Cab Calloway the way they all treated him.

I met Hobie, a friend of Hayes' and Franklin's who wore

33

dark glasses all the time, told great jokes, and carried a gun under his jacket. (Franklin told me he'd killed a couple of guys and he wasn't even in the war.) When the three of them had business together, I'd have to sit at another table and listen to the juke box for hours. It got so I hated the cokes they fed me while they talked, and Franklin let me order a scotch with a lot of water and ice.

Harlem was a thousand Franklins. I mean, loose, on their own, going and coming whenever they felt like it, eating breakfast at four in the afternoon, going to sleep whenever they were tired, taking off or working when they wanted to; and everybody was in the numbers and the horsebook, raising hell when they won and having a time of it either way. I tell you, I got this fever, this Harlem fever, and I wished I'd been born a black kid, because it seemed to me that even the people who lived in some slummy streets, I mean, with garbage all around, or even those Franklin didn't like, the preachers and Communist talkers at streetcorners, were all doing it in liberty hall.

Once I tried to say something like that to Franklin and he gave me a dark look. He told me that when you're poor and shit on every way you look, you got to keep moving, singing, preaching, fucking, gambling just to give yourself notice you're alive and something better than the rats in the walls.

"Damn few of us jump out of the griddle up to Sugar Hill like Paul Robeson or to Connecticut like Madame Walker with a fortune from whitening skins and straightening hair. But as for the rest, no matter what happens outside—I mean, getting better jobs, living where we want to, and all the rest of that hot-air equality—Harlem's going to look like a bombed-out city someday. Like London where the V-bombs hit. But if ever they make a goddamn barnfire of the place, where are the poor going to sleep? On the streets like in India? It looks like May Day in the park and July 4 in

Coney Island to you, and some of us love the place because it's all we know and leech on it because it's easy to con the poor, but the sound of Harlem you hear ain't joy, man, or nigger beat; it's a handfull of hard cash and a bucket load of trembling."

Franklin asked if I could go into New York with him on Columbus Day, and I said sure. He told me he was staying overnight there and I'd have to make it back to Beachport by train. No sweat. I'd be ready whenever he was.

I knew in my gut that this was the day he was going to take me to Em's, a woman friend he told me about. I took a shower that morning, put on my new corduroy pants and black loafers with pennies stuck under the leather band. Believe it or not, as Ripley said, I even snuck a comb into my back pocket so I could get my lousy hair to look better than a cat's on a live wire.

Mom and Pop were a problem as usual. But I got an idea to tell them that Eddie Norris was given a couple of tickets to the Globetrotters at Madison Square Garden and he asked me to go with him. Since it was Columbus Day and no school or homework, why not?

Mom had another idea. Vice-President Wallace was making a speech in Long Island City that day and the papers said he was thinking about organizing his own party to run for president. She said it was time for me to get interested in politics. I said I was interested okay but couldn't I keep going to the Globetrotters until I was old enough to vote? To tell the truth, I had more than enough politics in my current events class, taught by a pretty nice bald-headed guy named Louis Lawyer. He was always against something or another, like the Pope, Churchill, the A-bomb. The kids said he was a Commie, which was a lousy thing to say in those days, and some parents got up a petition to fire him.

"In Europe," Mom said, "boys your age—"

"Come on, Mom. You're always bringing up Europe. Every time we don't like something you give us to eat, you say remember the starving children in Europe. I'm really sorry for them, Mom, and if it'll help I won't buy a hot dog at the Garden."

"Don't be so smart-alecky," she said. "People are starving over there."

I heard her; she was right and I was a dope. I said I was sorry and I was.

During all this Pop was thinking and he said, "I have a solution."

I smelled danger.

"Melvin can go to the Garden providing—"

I was sure of it.

"Providing I go along."

I almost broke in two, but Mom jumped in and said that Pop ought to set an example.

Pop smiled a little. "In that case, we'll share the work. I'll go to hear Wallace and Melvin'll go to the Garden."

"What kind of deal is that?" Mom said before I had a chance to thank Pop. "It's terrible. It's your duty, Saul—"

Pop got angry for once and said that when he was sixteen he had to work to support his parents and he'd promised himself that when he had kids they'd have more freedom than he had. I was ready to applaud him when he turned to me and said I'd better pick up my schoolwork or he'd change his mind about things.

"And I want you to come home right after the game," he said.

I said okay, I'd do it after we had a couple of cups of cocoa at the Orange Room, which is what we called Nedicks, knowing that could bring us to the last train to Beachport. (I mentioned cocoa because Mom thought I drank too much coffee and coke.)

Then I had to make it right with Eddie, who was a mama's boy, as I think I told you.

"I hate to lie," he said when I offered him money for the train and the Garden ticket and laid out the plan.

"Who you hurting?"

That stopped him for a while. "But what if they ask me if I ever lied when I go up before the Bar Association?"

"It'll be years from now. Who'll know?"

"I don't know. Maybe I'll remember. . . ."

"Hell, by that time you'd have lied a billion times."

"You're pretty cynical," he said.

"You're going to the game anyway. Or to the movies. All you have to say if my mother bugs you is 'Sure, we were there.' Is that too much to ask?"

He thought about it, sometimes not being fast on the take. "Okay," he said.

"You take the last train and I'll meet you on it," I said. "And you can tell me who won and how."

Eddie said yes but he wasn't happy. Christ, I'd hate to be in his court if he was the judge. I tell you, once you get bar-mitzvahed you're marked for life.

On the way into town in Franklin's car, he talked a lot about how great I was doing collecting policy slips for him. "You sure picked it up fast," Franklin said. "You're smart with percentages."

"I do okay in math," I said, which was true. Math was my best subject. History caught me up on dates and names. Grammar was even worse.

"When you get a little older, I'll turn more business over to you." He looked at me and I smiled. "I'm thinking of making a partnership with Hayes and with Hobie. They've got a good piece of territory in Harlem and I've tied up Beachport and Oceanside. We'll go fifty-fifty."

"How do you divide fifty by three?"

"It's fifty for me and twenty-five apiece for them."

I thought that over for a while. He wasn't telling me this just to hear himself talk, not Franklin.

"How you doing in your other subjects?"

The question bugged me, but I said, "Okay."

"I want you to do better than okay. You got to get into a good college. Maybe Harvard. That'll help you with law school."

"I don't want to go to college and become a lawyer."

He looked at me quickly like I'd said something bad. "I'm wasting my time with you, boy. You're not as smart as I thought."

He was angry and that scared me.

"You think I picked on you to turn you into a little white Franklin? I told you that couldn't be. Maybe I was crazy to think that in five, seven years you could be a smart lawyer and I'd have some bread put away to invest through you in legit things like downtown real estate, banks, Texas oil. You think I want to spend the rest of my life pimping, penny poker and pinball machines? I thought I had someone I could teach what I know about gamblin' and greed so we could use it in the legit big time. That's what it's all about, this country. Make a bundle. And keep the law on your side."

He sighed a couple of long sighs. I couldn't find anything to say.

"Well," he said after a while. "Vibrations can be wrong sometime."

I thought that the way things were going, things I heard about a war with Russia, the end of the world could come before I even got out of high school. Five, seven years was a helluva long time away. Forever. I'd rather be dead than lose Franklin. I could promise, couldn't I?

"Okay, Franklin. Don't get angry. I'll work at school like you said."

He looked at me again with those big black X-ray eyes of his. "I'll be on your tail, boy." And he didn't sound any easier. "And don't let me down, hear?"

We drove along Long Beach Boulevard without saying anything for a long time, Franklin chewing a cigarette. He didn't smoke but chewed about a pack a day. He turned the radio on to the sports news, listened a while, then switched it off. I could see that he was still steaming.

We were working toward the Midtown Tunnel when he said suddenly, "Remember I told you about my kid?"

Something was coming I wouldn't like. I felt it like a pebble in my shoe.

"I'm thinkin' of bringin' him up to live with me."

I knew it! He'd have his own kid and I'd be back playing volleyball on the beach or at the Y.

"That's great," I said, pushing my voice to sound sincere. "I thought your wife didn't want him around you."

He swung the car past a truck when he shouldn't have. I knew he was spooked at something. When he wasn't in Harlem, he drove real careful.

"I got me a lawyer. . . . He says he gonna go to court and get visitin' rights."

What would that do to us, me and him, if his son, my age, moved in? Twice I tried to say something like "That'll be nice" but my throat got all chunked up and I couldn't even breathe easy.

"Maybe the two of you could get to be friends," he said.

I coughed a couple of times and he gave me a sideways look.

"Yeah," I said after getting the stuff in my throat cleared.

"What's eatin' ya, boy?"

"Nothin'. . . ."

"Somethin' chewing at your guts?"

"No, sir."

"Feelin' the greens?"

"What's that?"

"Oh, man, ya got learnin' to do. That's jello-sea! Think Brian goin' to be competition, eh? Take Daddy Franklin outta your hands, eh? Hell, boy, no one got me in their hands, y'hear? I'm Mr. Himself, by himself. Ain't no chains on me. Like I tell chicks when they're scratchin' at me. 'Get outta my mouth. I ain't nobody's dog. Let the air flow 'tween us. Hear? Or you'll have to get yourself another hustle.'"

I didn't say any more and he went on talking about how people tried to eat into him. "Commies and butter-talkin' preachers, all for the betterin' of man, come suckin' around Mr. Gilboa for handouts. Yellin' for the poor. Yellin' for heaven. And then there's the great I Ams. Black man got to get his dignity back. Hell, I'll buy all the raffle tickets they got and read their throwaways. They say they're leadin' us out of Toilets for Colored Only into the equality land. They can wipe their asses anywheres they want to, it's okay with me. I loved them all from Marcus Garvey and Father Divine to the Reverend Powell, who says he's gonna be president someday. And this new Abe Lincoln, Elijah Something-or-Other. But I tell ya this, boy, if I ain't told ya already. My black brother ain't gonna be any better than the whiteys. The light ones gonna stick their tongues at the coal blacks, and them that praise the Lord on Sunday or make speeches on 145th Street about Russia will be cheatin' on their wives on Monday or connin' some poor Mississippi nigger come up to the promised land with fifteen bucks and a yen to make a hundred so he can bring his folks up after him. The poor bastard'll end up in an alley because some tight-ass brother's mugged him to buy a snipe of horse. Everyone's for the party of Me and Now. That's humanology too! I'm not runnin' in any way but my own. No one's gonna put cuffs on my hands. Are ya listenin', boy? Any runnin' I'm gonna do is on top of the world, over the heads. I want space all around me!"

He grinned and hit his hand against the wheel. "Damn, I feel good!"

He was high on the preaching to me. I was glad of it too, because I'm a quick learner and I guess I needed someone to get me clear about things. He wasn't Pop putting notions in my head about how good everybody was except the Nazis.

I'd already noticed that when he was high—like at that time or when we would go to an afterhours club with maybe Basie or Calloway jamming—he'd lose his college-type way of talking and get niggerish, as he put it to me once. He'd swing his body along with the beat, clapping hands, laughing, yelling "Swing it, daddy! Sugar it, man!" Once he left the table when Ellington was jamming "Take the A Train" and sashayed toward the bandstand, his tie down, shirt open to the waist, and jigged away like one of those colored kids who picked up pennies in front of the Hotel Theresa or the Chicken Shack. Seeing him that way made me love every colored man and woman I ever saw, hungry to be like them.

When I got to know him better I dared ask him about it. He was sitting in his velvet-covered chair in the Beachport place, smoking. "It's jus' a good sweat, boy. We're all black at times like that. But it ain' gonna stay. No more than conkin' the hair to get it smoothdown like the whites. It's all gonna go with the wind. The last of the past. We gonna be so friggin' respectable one of these days and so pony-proud of ourselves you'll only see whites doin' the jiggin' and the niggers waltzin' at the Ritz. Shee-it!"

4 That day we stopped off for the first time at the Red Dog Grill or, as Franklin called it, The Bar. It was a home place for him and he wanted me to be known there. He introduced me to the one-eyed bartender, John Hemingway, who wore a silver patch and claimed he'd lost his eye in a Naples whorehouse during the war. Franklin knew him in the Army and told me the eye was lost in the landing in Sicily.

"Junior here," Franklin said, "is a special friend of mine, and when I'm not around, or Hobie or Hayes, see that he keeps out of trouble. One beer and he's ready to fight."

We shook hands and John said okay, and from that time on whenever I came in he called me Junior and gave me a free beer.

Hayes and Hobie were there and the place was crowded with vets just out of the Army who were drinking it up like crazy. I was the only white in the place, and one fellow, drunk as hell, walked back and forth in front of our table, saying he'd had too many friggin' whites up his ass—he was a Marine—and that he'd come to Harlem so he wouldn't have to see any again, and what the hell was some ofay doing here? Franklin told him to beat it but the dope kept sticking it into me.

Well, after a few warnings which the vet was too pissed to hear, Franklin jumped up from the table like a lion and grabbed the guy's arm. Another vet, soused to the gills, jumped in with a knife. Hayes and Hobie rose up alongside Franklin, but he didn't need them. He kicked the guy with the knife in the balls, and as the guy fell Franklin picked him up and threw him against the other fellow. A split second later John Hemingway had both guys under his arms and threw them into the street. Franklin was breathing hard, his eyes terrible to look at, like broken glass, and I could see that he was working hard to get hold of himself.

"Damn niggers. They want to kill whites, why the hell don't they ask which white, when?" He slammed his fist on the table. "Only slaves kill without thinkin'. Can't they all get that into their cottonheads? The ofays in this country ain't the only ones gotta change."

He told Hobie and Hayes that no matter where he was, on the can or phone, or if he was late, someone had to keep an eye on me. "I don't want him hurt if some nigger has to get his rocks off on a whitey."

A couple of minutes later John Hemingway called Franklin to the phone, and when he came back to the table he looked as angry as before.

"There's a lousy little punk pushin' my street," he said. "Let's move our tails!"

I went with Franklin; Hobie and Hayes drove their own cars. We looked like a convoy speeding down Seventh Avenue. There wasn't a cop around and I got a bang out of the way we went through red lights. Nobody ever stopped Franklin in Harlem.

When we got to Solly's Barbershop on Seventh and 136th Street, where Franklin did most of his numbers in a back room, Daisy was out in the street waiting for us. She was the sleepy fat dame I'd seen at Hayes' place near Penn Station when I delivered the money. She said something to Franklin and pointed to a skinny colored fellow in a Navy peajacket who was talking to some kids at the corner. Franklin told Hobie to get hold of someone named Cohalan and walked to the pusher, with me shadowing him. He shoved the kids to one side and told the skinny guy to fuck off.

43

The guy didn't look scared. He said, "Yeah. . . ." Like that was an answer, but he didn't move.

Franklin reached over and took a small envelope out of the guy's hand.

"Hey! That's mine!"

One of the kids tried to grab the envelope from Franklin. Franklin held him off and said to the pusher in a quiet way, "I'm Mr. Franklin Gilboa. This is my street, punk, and if you lived around here you'd know it."

It began to crowd up around us and someone yelled, "Yeah, man! You tell 'em, Mr. Gilboa!"

"Okay, we'll split the bread," the pusher said.

"Who's the dealer?" Franklin said.

"How about it man? Fifty-fifty."

Franklin slapped him hard on the face. "No one, y'hear, is goin' to push drugs around here. Not on the streets. Not to kids. Not to anyone!"

People in the crowd yelled, "That's right! The man said it!" A woman screamed, "God bless you!"

The pusher tried to break away.

"You ain't goin' anywhere," Franklin said, keeping his hold on him. Hobie came through the crowd with a white cop. Franklin shoved the pusher into his arms. "Take him, Cohalan. He's all yours." And he gave him the white envelope. "Here's the evidence."

Cohalan smiled. "Thank you, Mr. Gilboa. We need all the help we can get." He put handcuffs on the pusher.

"Get movin', scum."

"How's the wife?" Franklin asked.

"Busy with the good ladies of St. John's," the cop said.

"Let me know when they have their next bazaar."

"Yes, sir. And she'll thank you for whatever you do," Cohalan said. He walked off with the pusher in front of him like a seeing-eye dog.

People around Franklin touched his coat and tried to shake his hand. He smiled and thanked them like he was the mayor.

"That cop's on my payroll," he said to me when we were by ourselves. "And the sergeant and lieutenant. We build up a nice arrest record for 'em. Now and then we even let 'em raid Solly's when no one's around with much cash. Keeps the City Hall heat off of 'em." He stuck a cigarette in his mouth and chewed the tip. "Damn pushers. Harlem's been mostly clean up to now, except the musicians and the whores. Got to keep it that way. Bad for Harlem. Bad for my business. Bread going into drugs is bread not going into numbers."

In Solly's he had his shoes shined, although they shone like mirrors. Sitting in the big chair, he greeted customers going in and out of the back room. "How did ya do, young lady? Great!" Or "Try tomorrow, Joe. There's always the right number for the right man!" People stopped to talk, to ask favors and advice. And he listened, as if there wasn't anybody else in the whole world but them.

After a while he looked at his watch, grinned at me across the room, and said, "Doc, up in arms! We're going to Em's to find us some sweet, sweet sugar."

I began to sweat cold, but I told myself to take it easy. Mustn't do anything to shame my friend.

When we got into the car I tried to keep my mind off what was coming and brought up the subject of his partnership with Hobie and Hayes. I said that if there ever was a disagreement and it was fifty-fifty, how could they make any decision? He said then they wouldn't make a decision.

"But it could be a good deal. Why don't you take fifty-one percent? You're the smartest around. That's worth one percent."

"Whoa, boy. You think that and I think that, but Hobie and Hayes maybe they don't agree with us."

"Tell them you want it for your son," I said without thinking.

He mummed up and we didn't say any more. We drove south down Seventh Avenue. I kept rubbing my belly. I was getting nervous. There was a sign advertising the Globetrotters at Madison Square Garden and I thought of Eddie going there. What if there was a fire at the Garden that night? Or at the movie, if that's where he went? I mean, what if there was and Eddie got burned? And I wasn't there. God, I'd feel lousy about Eddie getting hurt. I'd have to tell my folks the truth. They'd probably keep from raising hell with me because of what happened to Eddie, but that wouldn't help him any, would it? You sure get into a helluva mess when you lie. It's like being disloyal, as Franklin said, and you ain't worth the crap on a sheet of pink toilet paper. Guess you always have to hurt somebody if you lie, I mean, if the truth comes out.

We went down Central Park West. The trees still looked great, even if it was October, and all the kids were roller-skating. Everybody trying to get everything in before it snows, I guess.

"The little bastard," Franklin said, real sad.

"What?"

"My son. . . . He's in trouble. That's why I'm trying to get him up here."

"Gee, Franklin, I'm sorry to hear that," I said.

"Damn kid!"

I kept my trap shut. I could see he was hurting. When we got to Em's on 81st Street, my belly wasn't on my mind anymore.

Em's place was in a penthouse overlooking Central Park. We went up in a big elevator run by a white man who seemed glad to see Franklin and landed on the fourteenth floor at a thick wooden door with carving on it. A cute-looking white chick opened it and said hello to Franklin, who gave her a pat on the ass. Then we went through another door into a room bigger than I'd ever seen before. It was all white, rugs, walls, furniture and everything except the curtains, which were purple. I mean, the place was like some kind of white dream. It was so white it took me a minute to see it all. Jazz was coming in soft and there were some men sitting on the couches and chairs talking to girls who were all dressed in the kind of clothes you see at weddings. You know, long, shiny, low-cut so you could see a little of the tops of their boobs. A maid was passing around drinks.

Em came out of a side door of the big room, called out to Franklin, and they kissed each other as if they needed it. She was a very black dame, tall but mighty heavy. Not fat, understand, but she showed a lot of muscle in her shoulders and arms. The dress she wore was as black as her skin, and it was hard to see where one ended and the other began.

"This is my very good friend Doc," Franklin said. "I want him treated right. We're going to be partners someday. I'd like him to meet Vincy."

Em smiled in a way that made her face look almost motherly, but she wasn't that way at all. She grabbed my hand in hers and gave me a crunch until it hurt. "You're welcome, honey," she said in a deep voice. "Take a look around and talk to the girls." She called over to the maid. "Tell Vincy there's a friend of Franklin's I want her to meet." The maid went up the stairs and disappeared.

As I moved away I heard her ask Franklin how old I was, and he said old enough but not to let my height fool her. Then they went into another room.

When the maid came back and passed around drinks I ordered a Cutty Sark on the rocks and a little water, which was Franklin's favorite. With the glass in my hand I walked around the room, not talking to any of the girls, who were with johns. I waited for this Vincy to come out and pretended I was studying the pictures on the walls of apples and trees and funny-looking cut-up banjos.

"Hello," a voice said behind me and I turned. "I'm Vincy."

Well, what can I tell you? I used to dream about Mary Astor in *The Maltese Falcon* and Ingrid Bergman in *Casablanca,* and I've even got a signed photograph of Gypsy Rose Lee. Listen, even the models in my Uncle Jack's shop were dogs compared to Vincy. She was a mulatto, skin colored like vanilla ice cream in a chocolate soda. A light blue dress was cut down to you know where, and her eyes were the same color. Her hair was dark and cut close to her head.

"Hello," I said, hoping I was sounding cool and wishing she didn't hear the ice knocking against the glass in my hand.

"You're Doc," she said, and I didn't know how she sounded because my eyes got in the way of my ears.

I sort of followed her over to a two-seater couch, and she ordered the maid to bring her something called an orange blossom. "For vitamins," she said.

It was tough holding the drink and looking at her at the same time sitting next to me. Besides, I smelled her perfume. . . .

"You live in New York?"

"Yes—I mean, New York State. Long Island."

"It's very pretty there."

We talked like that, back and forth, real stupid things, and I kept wondering what I was supposed to do next. I'd finished the drink and taken another, but I wasn't feeling them at all.

"You haven't been here before, have you?"

"No. But—" She mustn't think I was dumb. "I get around."

48

Now and then a john would get up from a couch with a chick by his side and leave through the front door. That didn't help me any.

"Are you in business?"

"I'm with Franklin."

That kind of got to her because she put her hand on mine. I hoped she didn't notice that mine was shaking.

"He's a great guy," I said. "We go to all kinds of places together. You know Eppie's or the Red Dog Grill?"

She smiled, nodded, and looked at her tiny gold wristwatch.

"Would you like to go to my place?" she asked in a quiet voice. Mom would have thought she was very polite the way she sounded.

I nodded quickly, then I thought I was being too anxious. "Why not?" I said.

She got up and went over to Em, who had just come back into the room. I suddenly stopped shivering and I took a quick look at my waterproof Army watch. It was only four o'clock. Lots of time. The one thing I didn't want to do was hurry. Em waved me over. "Franklin said for you to enjoy yourself," she said. "Everything's taken care of." I was sure relieved hearing that, since I didn't know what I ought to do to take care of everything.

Vincy had put on a long black coat and took my hand.

"Have a good time, children," Em said as we left. I didn't mind her saying that. I knew she wasn't talking about going to a Jewish Center Purim dance.

5 Vincy's real name was Mabel Smith, but she called herself Vincy and whatever last name she picked up from movie stars and singers. Sometimes she was Vincy

Fontaine, sometimes Vincy de Havilland, sometimes Vincy Cagney because she said he was her ideal man. She grew up in Washington, D.C., was raped by an uncle when she was ten, ran away from home, worked her way through high school by selling at Woolworth's, made it with the manager and some of the customers, then beat it to Harlem, where she hung around the cafés and bars, met Franklin, and ended up at Em's. She had a way of speaking nice and soft and very polite, but when she made love she screamed. She was my first woman, and I went nuts over her.

"You were terrific, sugar," she said when we were both laying back.

Now you'd think that would come as no surprise to me considering what I've told you about myself, but I must admit that the first time she did a helluva lot of the work. Still, to be fair to Doc Henshel, I kept it good and going a long time, wanting to show her that she was with a fellow who'd been around. I know she blasted because when it happened she grabbed my arms, sobbed at first, then suddenly screamed and kissed me all over like I had done something wonderful.

I felt damned good.

It was nine o'clock when she got up, made coffee with rum in it, and brought it to the bed with some great oreo cookies. I hadn't had any supper, and I told her I was hungry, so she brought in some sliced meat and tomatoes. We ate on the bed like a couple of kids on a picnic.

"You can stay here all night," she said. "It's okay."

What could I tell my folks? Could I call them and say I was staying with Franklin? Not a chance. They'd never even met him. Could I say I was staying over with my Uncle Jack and Aunt Gussie? Nope! That would be too easy to check out. I was trapped.

"I don't think I can, sugar," I said. "But I'll be back tomorrow or the next day."

She put the dishes on the floor and lay down beside me. "Was this your first time?" she said. "Was it?"

There goes the problem of lying again. I had told Franklin that I still had my cherry. Had he told her or Em? I didn't like to admit it to Vincy. At the same time, I didn't want to lie to her.

After a while I said, "Kinda."

"Kind of what?"

"Kinda my first time. . . . I did a lot of hot necking."

She laughed, put her arm around me, and kissed me. "Sugar, you're great! You're terrif! You're a real man. Any time I'm around and you're there, you come to Vincy, hear?"

I forced myself to look at my watch. It was ten-fifteen. The last train to Beachport was eleven-twenty, and it would take me twenty minutes to get to Penn Station. I didn't want to leave. I wanted to stay there the rest of my life.

"How long have you known Franklin?" she asked me.

"A while. . . ." Talking about him was not the first thing on my mind.

"Franklin's my best friend," she said. "I'd have died without him."

She said that she and Franklin had shacked up when they met at one of the clubs.

"He taught me a lot," she went on, not seeing that I wasn't exactly enjoying it. "How to dress, for one thing. How to talk. You know, no 'ain'ts' and 'up yours' and 'oh, shits.' He was very strict with me because he thought I had class, and his whores had to have class. He—"

"What do you mean, 'his whores'?" I asked. "Don't you work for Em?"

"Franklin's got his own stable. Me and Rosemary and Opal. He brought us to Em's and he gets his cut."

Jesus, I thought, Franklin's sure in a helluva lot of rackets.

That's why maybe he wanted Vincy for me. One of his girls. Keep it in the family.

"He's my number-one man," Vincy said, hotting up. "I was no virgin, believe me, when we met. But I didn't know screwing from a traffic light. I was all there, up front, quicker than an alley cat. Didn't know how to make a man feel good, real good, not just all gismed out. He taught me how to please. Timing, he used to say, that's the thing with a good lay. Timing before you start, timing during, and timing afterward. Pays off better than a triple hit. And listening too. Men like to talk. Men like to hear themselves with a dame. To show off with no one around to cut them down. So he taught me how to keep my trap shut and pay attention, so the john thinks you don't have a thought in the world but what he's telling you." She rubbed her hand over her slim creamy chocolate belly. "I've gotten tips of a hundred bucks just for listening even when the john never took his pants off. 'Be a lady,' Franklin kept saying. 'Talk like one.' You know something, sugar? He made me read books and *Time* magazine and the *New York Times*, editorial pages and all. I got me a degree at his college."

I could hardly talk. This time it was the john who was listening.

After a while it got kind of boring, all this stuff about Franklin, so I said, "I guess I ought to be going."

"That's a shame, honey."

She got out of bed and started dressing like it was a fire drill. Just like that. I got my stuff on too.

"I'll take you where you have to go," she said.

"No. You go to sleep."

"I've got to get back to Em's."

"Gee, I figured you'd be tired," I said.

"Don't worry about me. I don't get real washed out until three, four o'clock. Holiday like this is big at Em's."

52

I tried to give her a smile, and I wanted to say that if she had to go, okay, business is business. Instead I heard myself say, "Gee, I wish you didn't have to." Kee-rist, I must've sounded like a soupy kid whose Mama just left him alone. She said I was sweet, which didn't help any.

When we got to the Long Island side of Penn Station, I didn't want to leave the cab and sat there like a dumb ox. Then before she had a chance to ask what was wrong, I threw my arms around her and kissed her hard. "I love you, Vincy," I said and ran out of the cab.

Good old Eddie Norris was hopping around in front of Gate 11. "I was worried you'd miss it," he said as we ran down the stairs, along the platform, and onto the train just in time. The car was filled with sleepy men and women and railroad workers in their overalls. I took the seat near the window even though I knew that Eddie wanted it, but you can't see anything at night anyway, can you?

Eddie gave me the dope I needed. The Globetrotters had won 110 to 89. Sweetwater was crazy. Played like a machine gun.

"Did *you* have a good time?" he asked.

How do you answer a question like that when you've gone through what I did? "Fine," I said.

"Tell me about it."

My head was popping around like a kid's balloon in a high wind. Tell him? I didn't even know how to begin to think about it.

"I got laid," I said.

"Wow!"

But, you know something, feeling the way I did about Vincy didn't seem like the most important thing. I mean, what I had was new. Like everything in my body was on the outside.

"How was it?" Eddie asked.

Suddenly I thought of Franklin in the sack with Vincy. And his having a son. They were all mixed up together.

I got up from the seat and ran into the can. It was probably the rum in the coffee that made me throw up.

"How was it, Doc?"

"Okay. . . ."

I had run over after school to pick up slips from Franklin at the shoeshine stand.

"Vincy liked you."

That was like telling Niagara Falls about water.

He gave me one of those tight-eyed looks like he was trying to get through to the spine.

"You want to see her again?"

I had a hard time keeping from yelling that nothing was going to keep me away from her. "Sure," I said.

"Good lay, huh?"

I don't know why but that hurt my feelings and I didn't say anything. He moved away to pick up a pile of slips, checking them out before giving them to me. I had a crazy idea that what went on between me and Vincy oughtn't to be talked about, even by Franklin.

He held the slips in his hand and I forced myself to look up into his face.

"Em told me that you're kinda stuck on Vincy."

My teeth hurt from holding my mouth shut, but I managed to say, "She's okay. . . ."

"You know she's a friend of mine."

"I know."

"And she has a lot of friends."

My lip began to bleed. I didn't know it until he reached over and wiped a drop of blood from my chin. "Cut yourself shaving this morning?" he asked. Which was a rotten thing to say because I hadn't begun shaving yet, and he knew it.

He handed me the slips. And some cash. "You got a couple of hits to pay off."

That was good news but it didn't make me feel any better. What I was really thinking about was that I'd take some dough I had and get over to Em's to Vincy and buy her a present.

"A first lay can mean a lot to a man," he said. "Can make him really sure of himself or make him worry all the time."

"I won't have to worry."

He smiled a little. "So Vincy told me."

Nobody has any business talking about things like that.

"Congratulations, Doc."

"Thanks. . . ."

"Depends on the chick too," he said. "Get one who doesn't know what's going on, you can get a lousy lay'll set you back. I wanted you to have the best."

"I think I'd better get going," I said.

Franklin put his hand on my shoulder. "Listen to me careful, kid. One thing you don't want to do, otherwise you lose a helluva lot of fun in life—don't, don't ever keep hanging your coat on the same hook all the time. Dig it?"

I wanted to say "Fuck you," but I mumbled "Yeah" and slipped under his hand and got on my bike to pay off the hits.

6 God, the days were slow as molasses at home and at school, but when I was with Franklin or Vincy, no matter where, they ran like Distribute, who broke the record of one mile, five and a half furlongs at Cincinnati, Ohio, when he was nine years old and carried just about my own weight of 109 pounds. (Mom was complaining about my weight because I'd gotten so tall all of a sudden.)

I was real punk at school but that had to do with things which I didn't like to think about, mostly on those days when I couldn't be with Vincy because she was busy or I couldn't get away. Besides, who cared how congressmen and senators were elected or about England and India and Palestine. That was okay for Eddie Norris and Marcy, who never gave up trying to make me interested in all those heavy things. I tell you, it was enough that I had to memorize the Gettysburg Address, the preamble to the Constitution, and the Declaration of Independence. And though Mom and Pop kept pestering me about my marks, Franklin liked to hear me roll out "We the people . . . we hold these truths . . . of the people, by the people, for the people. . . ."

"You stamp all that on your spinal column," he said, "and you got everything. Trouble is, where you going to find a place where they count?" He once told me he'd stopped believing when President Roosevelt died. He showed me a picture printed in a newspaper of him crying as the coffin rolled by. "I never cried before," he said. "And never since."

I guess you could say I was living a double life. But the part I lived at home and school was like I was half asleep. And that was okay too, because my folks didn't expect anything else from me, no matter what they said. It was all Marcy. I wanted to be with Franklin, where the action was, and I didn't care that Franklin was in the rackets. It was where I wanted to be because, believe me, you were never half asleep when you were with him.

Like the time on a rainy Saturday afternoon I was supposed to be with Eddie Norris at a double feature of *The Best Years of Our Lives* and *The Killers*. Instead I was sitting

56

in back of Franklin in a poker game in a big moving van that rolled slowly through the streets of Manhattan, up and down Seventh, Broadway to Times Square and back, along Fifth and Lenox. The fellow who owned the van, Chris Johnson, came up with the idea of it during some kind of trouble about gambling at City Hall. On the sides of the van was painted YANKEES MOVING COMPANY with an address and license numbers and everything. As long as the driver didn't run any red lights, no cop would stop it. And it was a big GM with a toilet, a bar, and even a bedroom if any of the players wanted to snooze or call up a broad to spend a little time with him to change his luck.

The game had been going on for about a day and a half when I got picked up at 72nd and Fifth Avenue, where Franklin told me to be at one o'clock. I got on a camp stool behind Franklin and watched him play. He was winning a lot. The chips were stuck in holes in the table so they wouldn't fall when the truck ran over a bump or had to stop short for traffic. He had a pile, believe me. There was only one other fellow left in the game, name of Till, tall and skinny, a sourpuss with a long nose and thick lips he was always wiping with a red handkerchief. Every time he lost a pot, he'd touch Franklin's discards as if he could tell if cheating was going on.

Chris Johnson kept the whisky glasses filled, though all I had was coke. Franklin must've been drinking a long time because he kept whistling between his teeth without stopping even though Till didn't like it and asked him to stop. They played five-card stud, and you had to open with twenty-five bucks. Franklin was a cool player. With every deal he'd smile a little as if he had four aces or at least a flush, and he bluffed only once out of four or five times.

A couple of hours after I got there, Till was going light on a couple of pots, then he won one and was clear. Both

Franklin and Chris called for the last deal. Till raised hell, but Chris said they'd agreed to stop after forty-eight hours. It was Franklin's turn to deal and he gave the deck to Till to cut. Till called for open cards. Franklin okayed that and dealt him a king, himself a jack. Till shoved in twenty-five bucks. Franklin met him and gave Till a ten and himself a three.

It was king ten against jack three.

Till passed and so did Franklin.

The bus gave a bad lurch and part of Till's drink splashed down the side of his pants. He didn't move or say anything. His eyes were on the cards.

Franklin gave Till a king and himself an ace.

Till breathed like he had a bad cold. The cards were Till's pair of kings ten against an ace jack three.

Chris picked up Till's glass and filled it.

"What's it going to be?" Franklin asked Till, who rubbed his mouth with the red handkerchief.

"You in a hurry?"

"Uh-huh." Meaning yes.

Till counted his chips, then divided the stack in thirds. He bet one of the stacks. Maybe a hundred bucks. Franklin raised him by fifty. After all, he was playing with Till's money. Till met him.

Till's next card was an eight, Franklin's a five. It was Till's game with his kings.

"This is the last game," Chris warned Till. The van stopped and the engine was turned off. It sounded funny without the noise. "We're back in the garage," Chris said.

Franklin stopped whistling and waited. He held his fingers about six inches away from the deck, as if he were afraid to touch it.

"Last card," he said, which was kind of foolish.

Till folded his handkerchief on itself and this time wiped the side of his sweaty nose, then he put his fingers behind his chips, rode them into the center of the table, and drank his whisky to the bottom of the glass.

Franklin's fingers inched up to the deck and flipped the top card. It was a four. Till still had his kings. Franklin was about to turn over his own card when Till put his hand with the handkerchief on the deck. "I'll deal it," he said, whispering.

"Don't trust me?" Franklin said.

"I said I'd turn the card," Till said. "Any objections?"

Franklin smiled, but I saw he didn't think it was funny. "I'm dealer," he said.

"I don't like the way you handle the deck."

"Late in saying so."

Chris broke in. "Let's get it over with. I'll draw the card."

"The hell you will," Till said.

"There's only one dealer and that's me," Franklin said. He reached for the deck, pushing Till's hand to one side, and turned over the top card. It was an ace. He had a pair of aces and the pot.

Till didn't say anything. His hands lay on the table like a pair of blackbirds with the red handkerchief in their beaks.

"Take your cut, Chris," Franklin said, bringing to his side of the table the mountain of chips. "And cash me out."

"Got me a new Caddie outside," Till said. "Free and clear. Bet you five grand against it. On one card."

"Got my own," Franklin said.

"Come on, man. You're holdin' my whole bank."

"Forget it." He got up, ran a finger around his shirt collar, and looked at his watch. "Christ, it's four-thirty. Come on, Doc, I'm hungry. Let's eat."

"Ain't gonna give me a chance at gettin' some of it back?"

"Brother, you had forty-eight hours of chance. Besides, you got nothing left to play with but a secondhand Caddie. Game's over and done with."

The look on Till's face wasn't something I liked, but the

whole thing was so goddamn exciting, I mean, nothing in the movies came near it. Franklin was so diggety sure of himself, on top of everything. I knew I was going to be like that when I was his age.

Chris paid off with a thick batch of hundreds while Till put on his overcoat slowly and stared at the money. He was still breathing like he had a cold. Then he left the van without saying a word.

Chris said that Till was an asshole and he wasn't going to let him play the van anymore.

"It's okay," Franklin said. He looked down at me as if I were the only person in the place. "What time you got to get back, son?"

"If I make a call around six or so I can maybe stay until the last train."

"Give Doc a Cutty Sark and water. Lots of water. We're going to have us a ball the next couple of hours."

Suddenly he wasn't tired anymore.

I don't know exactly how to tell you what happened next because things moved fast and I'm not sure how much I was seeing and how much I was feeling. I mean, I'm not a pro at telling things like Mr. Clothier, my English teacher, who could stand there on his two feet and tell the story of Julius Caesar in a way that almost made you smell the old goat's hair oil and hear the roar of the crowd when Mark Anthony said, "Friends, Romans, countrymen, lend me your ears." That's a helluva sight better than reading and even listening to the radio. Well, anyway, I'm not Mr. Clothier, thank God, and he ain't me, and all I can do is try.

The van was in a garage on 138th Street off Fifth, and when we left it was dark and a little rainy. Franklin grabbed my hand, and we cut through traffic across the street to Thelma's to get us something to eat. Thelma, a good-looking broad with thick glasses, made a fuss over Franklin. The Cutty Sark was getting to him and he talked more about himself than ever before.

"When I was ten I was like you, tall and skinny. Folks used to say I was the only nigger boy in Baltimore without a shadow. Hah! I had a shadow. Not thick but long, boy. Real long! I used to swear by the time I was twenty-one I was going to have me a thousand bucks. Took me a little longer, but hell, Doc, I got ten of 'em in my pocket right now. Oh, man! More warmin' than a pair of grapefruit-sized tits is ten grand. . . ."

We were eating Thelma's special—thick pea soup with lots of ham in it. Real good stuff. Not like my Mom made. Hers always had too much salt and not enough peas. Or the other way around.

"Yes, sir, when I was about twelve I went to work for a pickpocket named Cross-Eyed Charlie. We used to work Yankee Stadium, the Polo Grounds, Madison Square Garden. And the tracks. Jamaica, Bowie—all of them. He was so cross-eyed the marks never knew which way he was looking and he'd have their stash quicker'n a fly on new horseshit, right into my pocket. And me with my nice clean pickaninny mug, dressed so clean you'd think I'd just come out of Macy's Boys Shop. Anybody took a notion I was in on the con and put a hand on me, he'd have the cops on him for molestin' a minor. Hah! What days!"

What days! God, when I was twelve all I had was parchesi, lectures on keeping my room clean and saying please and thank you, movie shows on Saturday, and a snotty sister who was the queen of the Henshel family because she was already in third-year high at fifteen, a member of the Scholastic Honor Society, and had a letter printed in the *New York Times* praising Winston Churchill. And I'll never forget having to dress up in white duck pants and walk up and down on the boardwalk with Pop and Mom in the summer.

"You know what I'm going to do with all this bread? I'm going to find my Mama," Franklin went on. "Ain't seen her in years. When my Papa died, she just up and flew, leavin' me with an Auntie. . . ." He took a big gulp of Cutty and stared out the window behind me. "I'll find her, and I'll hang thousand-dollar bills on her from titties to toes and back again."

Never thought—and I know this is crazy—but I never thought of Franklin having a mother. He just seemed to be made by himself, the way I think of myself sometimes. You know what I mean, like we came into the world without anybody's groans, grunts, or help. My friend, least of all. Truth is I didn't ever think of him as a kid.

"Grew up with the rats on Calvert Street," he said, dreaming over his whisky and chewing cigarettes. "Then Auntie took me to Harlem to live with her and a longshoreman named Big Jack Dempsey. A puny cat but strong as Lionel Strongfort. Auntie and Big Jack used to hang around the clubs doing odd jobs, and I got to hear all the greats. Louie, Pearl, Billie Holiday, Basie, Cab Calloway, and lots of fellows you never heard of and never will but they was greater than the great. Booze, drugs, and pussy beat most of 'em down. And then there was the no-money blues. Christ, Doc, they'd work for the shells of peanuts at Small's, the Cotton Club, the Apollo, even the Regent Theater way down in white Harlem where the Jews used to come on Friday nights and dig all that stuff like it was Jerusalem music."

He finished his drink, called for another, started to laugh, and stopped. "I'd have been a trumpeter myself if I hadn't had these broken thumbs. . . ." He fingered the bumps like they were rat poison.

"I knew I wasn't goin' to be shit-poor all my life, boy.

Question was how to make it without puttin' on the chains. Worked for a pimp when I was your age. Never wanted to hurt anybody. Pimping don't hurt. You help your fellow men get their rocks off and chicks make a fair livin'. I know, man. It's the system. Get as much for as little. Got busted now and then. Fellow, a white fellow, swung me around. He was a Jew like you, boy. NAACP lawyer. Made me walk the red-white-and-blue line till I got me one year at New York University. That was in thirty-six or something like that. He disappeared one day, this Sidney Traube. Found out later he went to Germany to save some Jewish folks from Hitler. Never came back."

He told me a lot and I tried to keep it all in my head. I know I'm not telling even a smitch of it. He had to go to work after his first year at college and couldn't find anything other than running a night elevator in a clothing-makers' building on lower Broadway. Not enough to get the dirt out of his mouth until he had a chance to run policy back in Harlem.

"And I kept on lookin' for Mama," he said. "Used to hang around the whitey apartment houses thinking she was doing maid work. Never found her." He slammed a fist on the table angrily. "I will, damn it. One of these days. . . ."

He was quiet for a while and I thought he'd never get out of his chair, he'd drunk so much. Then he said almost in a whisper, "I told you about humanology, Doc. It means you don't hurt anybody. Right? It means you don't go for sellin' horse or facepowder. It means you work the odds in your favor, but you pay off. It means you gotta build yourself. Keep your space. . . . See a guy slip on the ice, you help him up. Say 'Never mind' when he thanks you. Walk off without taking his name and address. He give you a buck, take it. Do you as much good as it'll do him. But you don't start connectin'. You're your own man, hear, Doc? That's the only system aroun' worth havin'. Humanology." He stood up and yelled for his check. "You know what I'm talkin' about, Doc?"

I said yes, but I wasn't sure I dug it all.

"Humanology! Don't forget!"

Franklin was ready to go. That was like him. No sleep for forty-eight hours or more but busting out to get going somewhere to do something. "We're going to Em's, old Doc," he yelled. "Do a little rockabye-babying. I got me a new broad up there. Name of Idabelle. I'll have me a tumble. What d'ya say?"

I didn't say anything. I just hoped that Vincy was free. I hadn't seen her more than twice the last ten days or so.

The drizzling outside was heavier. I followed Franklin into an alley alongside the garage where the van was parked. It smelled of cat piss. There was a street lamp at the other end next to his Caddie.

When we were about halfway there Till came out from behind a high pile of old tires. He had a gun in his hand and he was inches away. "Okay, you cheatin' sonuvabitch," he said. "Let's have my bread back."

Franklin stopped and started to reach into his overcoat.

"Keep ya hand right there," Till said. "You, punk—" He was speaking to me and I shivered a little. "You get his wallet."

"I won fair," Franklin said.

"Bullshit," Till said.

I didn't know what to do. I was shaking good. The lousy rain was getting inside my collar.

"Do what the bad man tells you, Doc. It's his gun."

I put my hand inside Franklin's coat. The side pocket. His heart was beating fast. Like mine. I took the wallet out.

Franklin grabbed it from me. "I'll take out my stake," he said and opened it. Then before I knew it he slammed his fist down on Till's arm, knocking the gun to the street. With his left hand he cracked Till across the mouth. I ran to pick up the gun and gave it to Franklin, who put it in his coat.

Till was bent over a little, making a sound like a kid whining for a glass of water before going to bed. Franklin wiped the rain off the wallet and stuck it back in his pocket.

Till stood up slowly. He stopped whining and his lips moved like he was sucking in air. The rain fell off his hat onto his chin. He wiped his mouth.

I never saw a real man hit before, not counting the movies. Till looked like he was crying but it was probably the rain.

"You—gonna—hear—from me again," Till said, getting out every word slow, like he was too cold to talk.

"Listen to the man, Doc. He's threatening me. 'Hear from you?' Man, you got nothin' to say to me. You're a big fat zero in Harlem from now on. Beat it. Find yourself a racket in another city."

"Ya better sleep with an eye open," Till said.

Franklin began to laugh in a crazy drunken way. It really scared me.

"Hell," he said. "I don't plan on spendin' the rest of my life worryin' about you, man. When I sleep, I wanna close both eyes and sleep hard. Can't enjoy life watchin' for shadows."

He took Till's gun out of his pocket and gave it to him. *Gave it to him!*

Till held the gun like it was the end of a burning firecracker. His other hand wiped his eyes.

"I told ya I ain't gonna live that way. Ya got your gun. Use it. Use it now."

Franklin had his hands behind his back.

God, I was scared.

Till was breathing hard. He held the gun and stared at

Franklin like he was looking right into the sun. Then without a word he stuck the gun in his pocket, turned, and sloshed through the puddles toward the street light.

My throat ached with wanting to tell Franklin how great it was being his friend, but I couldn't say a thing except "Crazy. You're one crazy man. . . ."

He turned up the collar of his overcoat. "Let's get to Em's and have us some dried clothes, boy."

When we got into the car, he let the motor run for a while to warm it, wiped his hands and face with a towel from a compartment under the dash, and put on his gloves.

"I'da been crazy if I let him spook me," he said. "Can't live that way."

"But he coulda killed ya!"

"The odds were with me." He gave that laugh again. "Take Hobie, for instance. He ain't got a worry in the world. Could kill a guy in cold blood. I figure that sore losers ain't sure enough of themselves to do it. Yep, there's some that can and some that can't."

He turned on the radio. A news program about riots in Palestine. He switched to the racetrack results.

"Feelin' okay, boy?"

I had to clear my throat a couple of times. "Yes, sir!"

Vincy wasn't at Em's—she was out on an all-night trick—and that griped the hell out of me. Em got me another girl. But the truth is I hated it. I wanted Vincy and no one else. I couldn't get anything going for me. I didn't know why.

I got home okay on the last train and there wasn't any fuss in the house, except the usual with Marcy. Didn't get much sleep either, fighting between thinking of Vincy and of how close Franklin came to being killed. I loved them both, and I wished I had the guts to do what he did.

7 Well, I guess nobody likes to talk about things that hurt, except operations in hospitals. I went into town to be with Vincy as many times as I could, and the times she wasn't there griped me, you can believe it! One afternoon when she and I were in bed together in one of Em's private rooms smoking maryjane—Vincy taught me how to roll the sticks—she said, "Why do you look so grumpy, sugar? Didn't I give you a good time?"

"That isn't it, Vincy."

"Tell your sweet mama."

I didn't want to say anything. It's like that sometimes. So much tries to bust out of your brain you can't find the space to let it through your mouth. She lay next to me, her cocoa skin beautiful on the pink sheets. The fingers of one hand cupped her breast and the other lay against my thigh. She knew how to turn a fellow on. Part of me was dizzy with Vincy and part of me was thinking of the johns she had laid that day maybe. Certainly the day and night before. She told me once she would turn six tricks in a day. Lying there next to her with the johns on my mind, I could feel a real crazy growing inside me.

"Damn it, Vincy! Why don't you leave Em's?"

She laughed a little and that didn't help me any. "Do what, honey?"

"I'll take care of you!" I rolled over on top of her.

"Golly, golly. . . ."

"What the hell does that mean?"

"It means you're shootin' off your sweet mouth but you're not makin' sense."

I put my arms around her and nuzzled her boobs like a baby. "Vincy, Vincy. . . . It hurts like hell. I love you. . . ."

"Man, I love you too."

"Then how can you take on all the other johns?"

"Oh, Doc boy, how you think I make me a nice living?"

"But if you love me—"

She ran her fingers across my cheek. "What's one thing got to do with another? I love you because you're a man where it counts. And you're young and ain't—aren't—spoiled and you treat me nice. Hell, you get me over the hill like nobody else."

"If I had lots of bread, you'd go with me."

She pulled her hands away and sat up. "Not if you had a million."

"Why not?"

"Because I like what I'm doing."

I hit her. My God, I hit her. Not hard, because halfway there I tried to pull my arm back. But there it was right on her cheek.

She jumped out of bed and ran to the wall mirror to look at her face, then to the can.

I ran in after her. "Vincy, I'm sorry! I'm sorry!"

She was wetting a washrag in the cold water and pressing it against her cheek. "Gotta keep it from swelling up."

"I couldn't help it, baby."

I stepped away. I could see her great body in the mirror, everything on it just right like a picture puzzle put together.

"Vincy. . . ." I wanted to get down on my hands and knees and beg her to forgive me, but I was ashamed of doing anything as childish as that so I decided I'd better beat it before I went crazy again.

"Where you goin'?" she asked and her voice was tough.

68

"I don't know."

She had her arms and legs wrapped around me. I mean, she was climbing up my body, breathing hard and saying, "Let's get with it, man!"

I didn't dig what it was that creamed her but she was a wild woman, and it didn't take long before she screamed that scream of coming which made me die and come to life again. When it was over she took a silver box the size of a quarter out of her pocketbook and gave it to me.

"What's it for?" I asked after I thanked her.

"For pills."

"Hell, I'm never going to take pills."

"Yes, you are. Someday."

"I don't like pills."

She smiled and kissed me.

"How about tomorrow?"

She patted her hands together like a baby. "You're the mostest, honey."

"Well, what about it?"

"Going away to Palm Beach tomorrow. Franklin's arranged something for me and Idabelle. A yacht. Some high-livin' johns. Politicians, I hear. Big money. I'll buy you what you want down there. What do you want?"

"Go to hell!" I yelled and put my clothes on in a hurry. I wasn't going to be made fun of. God, I hated her. And Franklin. I threw the silver box on the bed and told her where to stick it. I wanted to call her a lousy whore. But she'd only say, "That's what I am, honey." I wanted never to see her again and I wanted not to let her go. It's hell having two feelings like that at the same time.

But I counted the days, and when Em told me Vincy was back I bought her a red scarf at Ohrbach's made of silk without telling Franklin and gave it to her when we were together again. She said she was glad to see me, and for a couple of hours I didn't think of the Florida trick.

8 It was sometime in January or February when things blew up in the house with Pop and Mom, and I wasn't ready for it. I'd had a lousy week, flunking current events and just skinning by European history from 1815. Current events really threw me. Gandhi had just been killed, I mean, just a week or so before the finals. It never came up in class because we didn't meet that week, and the whole stupid test was one question: "How did the death of Gandhi affect the relationship between India and the rest of the world?" How do you answer that if you never heard of the Indian fellow except what Mom said about him, that he was a great pacifist? I did my damnedest to signal for help from Eddie, who was sitting in the row alongside me, but the teacher, a fellow who was always criticizing the government, kept walking up and down the aisles like he was looking for the key to the atomic bomb. And I was all set for questions on the UN and the Palestine partition plan.

What made the week even worse was that I could get to Em's only once and Vincy was sick.

I think I told you about some money I'd made with commissions and a couple of lucky bets at the track with Franklin. (God, I sure loved horses. Someday I was going to own a few and get myself in the winner's circle. There's something about the way they look, real good racehorses, that makes you think they got their own world by themselves and you'd better treat them right.)

Well, this isn't just to boast but to explain how I happened to have about a hundred bucks inside an old tennis shoe stuck under my bed. I didn't know what to do about all that jack. Buy clothes like Franklin? My folks'd be on me with questions that'd make Mr. District Attorney sound like the Bobbsey Twins, which, believe it or not, was the first book I read. And how much can you spend on buying cokes, frosted chocolates, and strawberry sundaes for Eddie Norris and the gang?

Even there I had to be careful, because if the word got around that Doc Henshel was buying at Goldberg's Drugstore sooner or later someone would hear about it—like, for example, Danny Calagero, who worked there and who was a friend of Marcy's and just as dumb-smart as she was. And if Marcy knew, it would go by Western Union to Mom. . . .

But then the blast came. It was a Sunday morning. Pop was having a late breakfast because he felt a cold coming. Marcy was reading the *New York Times* Book Section and oohing and ahing about some stupid book. Mom was already finished and was sitting at the end of the table staring at me like an overweight J. Edgar Hoover. I was halfway up to the mouth with a glass of orange juice when she said, "Where'd you get it?"

I looked around, thinking she was talking to Pop or Marcy.

"You. I'm talking to you."

"Me?" I already smelled something in Denmark.

"Where'd you get it?"

"Get what?"

"Don't lie to me. You know what I'm talking about."

I could have said, "What're you talking about?" and there'd be more stupid questions and answers. But there are some things where you have to go with your gut, like Franklin with Till, jump the other fellow, get to the point before he's there, and work up the odds. Pop blew his nose, making me want to feel sorry for him, but I didn't feel sorry for anyone at that time but myself.

"You talking about the money that I had under the bed?" I honestly felt innocent right then and there.

"What else?" Mom asked. "How you slept maybe?"

"You mean that I was saving to buy the family birthday presents with?"

Marcy put down the paper and gave me a look like a slice of lemon. If I'd said the earth was square she couldn't have believed me less.

"That's very nice," Pop said suddenly. I could always count on him working both sides of the street.

"Thanks, Pop."

"A hundred dollars. That much you don't save out of fifty cents a week spending money," Mom said, and I was right back where I started from.

"I worked for it."

"Cleaning streets, no doubt," Marcy said.

"You shut up!"

"Fooling around with that colored fellow," she said. "What do you do? Shoot crap every afternoon?"

"A lot you know about Mr. Gilboa!"

"I saw you at his shoeshine stand after school."

"We were talking about sports."

"And I saw you get into his car last Thursday."

"So he wanted to teach me how to drive."

"I don't want you driving automobiles," Mom said, like it was the crime of the century. "You'll wait until you're old enough to get a license."

"But how did you make a hundred dollars?" Pop asked, crossing the street. I think I could've told him everything, but I know you can't do that with parents. The trouble is that they're always thinking of when they were kids when they didn't know an A-bomb from horse manure, which is what they called it then.

72

"Well, about the money," I said, knowing that we'd come to the fourth down, ten to go, and ten seconds to play. "I bet on horses at Jamaica and I won."

"Hah!" That was Marcy, my friend.

"I told you, Saul, we should've put our foot down with that colored man," Mom said, dumping on Pop as if he had stood between her and the end of the world.

"You went to Jamaica on schooldays?" Pop said.

"Only once. The rest of the time on Saturdays."

"You had a long shot?"

I said yes and mentioned a few of the winners, which I didn't have but who would know?

"How did you figure out your bets?"

"I got to study the *Racing Form*."

"For that he has time," Mom yelled. "For gambling and tracks and horses, he can find time to study. For books, like Marcy, no. Have you read *The Tale of Two Cities*, which you're supposed to read over the Christmas holidays?"

I said I read it in *The Book of Knowledge* and who has to read a million pages to know the story?

"Your father'll take charge of the money," Mom said, "and there'll be no more horse betting."

"It's my money!"

"When it comes time to go to college, you'll be able to use it. We don't need such expensive presents. And further, you will not see that colored man anymore. You'll come home from school every day. That's my final word!"

I was on my feet before I knew it. "He's my friend!"

"He's years older than you. How can he be your friend?"

"He is!"

"I'm not going to have my son a racetrack tout!"

"I'm going to see him!"

"Saul?"

She called on Pop to take the rap, but I wasn't listening to anybody.

"I don't care," I said. "I'll run away!"

"Big shot," Marcy said, whispering.

God, she had no heart that sister of mine.

Mom began to cry. I can't stand anybody crying, me least of all, and there I was tasting tears in my mouth like a goddamn baby. After a while I looked at Pop, who was blowing his nose again.

"Where'll you sleep—on the beach?" Marcy said.

"Be quiet, Marcy!" That was Pop coming to life at last. "Melvin isn't going to run away."

"But he isn't going to see that *schwartzer* either!" Mom said, wiping tears from her eyes with the back of her hand.

"You don't like colored people?" I asked.

"I have no prejudice. I'm a member of the NAACP."

"Then stop calling them *schwartzers!*"

"What's the matter with the word? It means 'black.' So they're black."

"You don't like to be called a kike."

"It's not the same," Pop said.

"It's the same." I wasn't sure, but I felt I was right.

"So go live with the blacks!" Mom said.

"Anna, that's not right."

"Go, talk to your horsetrack son, don't talk to me."

Pop stood up. He was trembling. I could see the handkerchief in his hand move up and down. "We've had enough for today. I'll think about what we should do. Until then, Melvin, I want you to stay away from Mr. Gilboa." His voice became louder than I'd ever heard it before. "You understand, you'll do as I tell you."

It's no fun to see your own father—who never spoke much and, when he did, was quiet about it—suddenly become Hitler. Besides, he was catching a cold. I felt sorry for him and left the table.

I was in my room for a couple of minutes when I suddenly

74

remembered that I hadn't had any breakfast. But I wasn't hungry and the hell with it. I wasn't going back into the dining room with Marcy and Mom and Pop sitting like some weird judges. I was going to run away for sure if they made me swear I wouldn't see Franklin again, not that I couldn't have sworn and then lied. Heaven wasn't going to open and give me a kick in the ass. I stopped believing in God a long time ago, around my tenth birthday. I don't remember exactly how it happened but my folks were talking a lot around that time about what Hitler was doing to the Jews, and somebody, maybe Uncle Jack and Aunt Gussie, who were having supper with us—they're my cousin Diana's parents—said something about God and Mom got up from the table, it was Friday night, and she put her fingers right in the flames of the candles which we always had on Friday nights and squashed them out and screamed at the top of her lungs, "No more talk about God! There is no God! Anybody who thinks there's a God is a moron!"

Pop shushed her, saying, "Anna, the children!" But he couldn't stop her and she put her arms around Marcy and talked like a crazy woman. I didn't get what she was saying but I began to cry because I hated to see her that way. It was real frightening. Not that it was a big deal not to believe in God. Pop and Mom never did much about it, except Friday nights with candles, and Passover.

But the rest of the time, whenever Marcy brought the subject up—she was always bringing up heavy subjects—the folks talked about ethics, whatever that meant, but God wasn't part of it, so He kind of faded away. Of course, they claimed we were Jews, which was okay with me since almost everybody in the neighborhood was Jewish, although what the hell that meant I didn't know or much care. Once when Eddie Norris tried to talk me into getting bar-mitzvahed with him because we were born Jews and we had to do it considering all the Jews who were killed by Hitler, I told him I was sorry as hell for them but the only thing I was born with was the little pisher that made me a man and not a lousy girl. The rest was for the birds.

So maybe I wouldn't have to run away. I'd lie to see Franklin. That wasn't such a big deal either. It's the only way to get on in the world, I mean, except being honest like Franklin in the rackets. Be loyal to your friends. Pay what's due. Pay on time. Never renege! Never!

I lay on the bed and gave my room the onceover, thinking how funny it is that you can live in a place your whole life and not really see what's there. I must have walked on the carpet a million times and I couldn't have told you what color it was until that morning. It was a dirty blue. And the bookcases with kid books last seen by me maybe at the age of ten. Except *Guadalcanal Diary* and a couple of paperback novels Marcy tried to cram down my throat. I gave the walls a hard look. A silly red pennant from Atlantic City, a war poster of an American pilot drowning and the words SOME-ONE TALKED, which, believe it or not, almost turned me on to wanting to join the Air Force when I got old enough.

The truth is I wasn't crazy about running away, although I was sure Franklin would fix up something for me. It's that I hated making a lot of people unhappy, Pop and the rest. I just wanted to be left alone, that's all. Left alone to do what I wanted. I couldn't see how that hurt anybody.

It's hell having nothing to do but read and listen to the radio on a Sunday morning when there's nothing on but stupid sermons. The pro-football games didn't begin until later.

I found an old parchesi set and rolled the dice for an hour or so, trying to figure out the odds on throwing sevens if I started the roll with sevens on the dice. But I got nowhere. Now and then I heard Marcy in the can showering and dry-ing her hair. She had a date every Sunday with this Garagola fellow, a jockstrap soph at NYU, and she deserved him. God, I can't stand people who think books and college degrees are the way to live. They go to concerts!

If I told Pop I'd been helping Franklin with the numbers, he'd say it was against the law and I'd have to get into a big argument about all the hypocrites who break the law every day and get away with it. Like the people in my family who bought black-market meat during the war. Or cheated on the ration stamps. My Pop and Mom with all the others. Like Franklin said, you can be crooked in a legit business and honest in the other kinds. No use wasting your life worrying about what's right and wrong just as long as you don't hurt anybody.

All that thinking and no breakfast gave me a headache, so I tried to work up a little excitement in my head about Vincy. I don't enjoy getting off on myself because there's no fun in it. What I mean is that you're laying there in a puddle and not feeling anything but disappointed and wet. Even before I met Franklin I'd decided to give it up. I didn't need him to tell me that I was wasting time. What a lousy thing it would have been not to get screwed before the A-bomb fell!

I didn't hear Marcy come in until she was alongside the bed.

"I didn't want to wake you," she said.

"I was awake."

"Listen, Melvin—" She could make that shitty name sound like a funeral march. "You know the folks have only your best interests at heart."

You'd think she was too smart to give me that crap. But I let her go on. Sometimes you have to let the animals run free.

"You want to make something of yourself, don't you? I know you don't care what I say, but that's natural. Kid brothers and older sisters are always fighting. Sibling rivalry is a normal situation in families. Now, I've got nothing against colored people. You know that we're all mixed blood. Jews like us have got a thousand strains. Who knows how many, way back, intermarried or got raped and had Cossack children. And before then, when we lived in Spain and the Moors were around. So it's foolish not liking colored people. It's not the color but the kind of people you have to worry about. Racetrack touts, gamblers, gangsters. White or black, Italian, Jewish, Irish, it makes no difference. We are all the family of mankind. But I don't want my brother to get in trouble because of his associates."

She went on like that with her college talk, telling me what I should do and not do, and I kept looking at her face trying to figure out how we could be related when we were so different. Her hair was blondish, mine was black; her eyes were like the Chinese, not round like mine; her skin was dark and her nose was long and thin and mostly shiny. I mean, how different could you get? At school some of the gang called me a mick because I had black hair, blue eyes, and a turned-up nose. Could one of us be adopted?

"You aren't listening!" she said, sounding like Mom.

"I am! I am!"

"You know what the trouble with you is? You want to be everything I'm not!"

She was right there.

"Because I love to read, you hate books. Because I'm going to make something of myself, you want to be a bum. Because Pop and Mom are proud of me, you want them to be ashamed of you. Isn't that it?"

"Shit!" I said.

"That's it? That's the best you can say when I try to be reasonable with you?"

"Ditto."

78

"You're running away from the world, Melvin. You don't care for anything or anybody but yourself. You don't even care about the future of the world."

She was wrong there, okay. I cared a helluva lot about the future, but I sure didn't want to be caught up in it before I had my chance at bat.

"You don't even care about the Jews from all those concentration camps. And what about the problem of the veterans coming home?"

She wasn't helping my headache, and I said it was a bad time to tell me what I should care about when I hadn't had any breakfast. Well, that got to her. She let go with a right and slapped my face. I grabbed her around the middle and threw her on the bed and then stepped away because I didn't like to fight with girls, even sisters.

"You're a bastard," she said, jumping off the bed and trying to catch her breath.

"That's a lousy insult to Pop and Mom," I said.

She ran to the can and slammed the door so hard the war poster fell off the wall.

I guess I must've really slept this time because I woke up to the sound of a radio coming from an apartment across the areaway that separated our building from the next one. Some highbrow stuff that was on every Sunday afternoon over WCBS the same time as the pro-football games. I got up to close my window when Pop came in. He had a tray with a couple of sandwiches and a glass of tomato juice.

"I was in before," he said, "but I didn't want to wake you."

I never had meals in bed except when I was sick and I said thanks, really meaning it. He picked up the war poster, stuck it back on the wall, then sat down in a camp chair with DIRECTOR painted on it that I stole from the Jewish Center.

They put on shows there, and the folks used to make me go when I was a kid. I hated all the stuff about Queen Esther and the Maccabees, and I got even one time by swiping the chair. The funny thing is that no one in my family ever asked me where I got it. That shows you that parents always worry about the wrong things.

Pop sat there watching me eat and saying nothing. I suddenly remembered how he and Mom sat by my bed when I had pneumonia. All night too. They told me later I almost died but I didn't remember about that. Just that they sat there holding my hand and wiping the sweat from my face. They were in their bathrobes all the time, and whether I was dreaming or not I don't know, but I thought I saw them kiss each other once after they took my temperature. God, parents'll do anything for you when you're sick but once you're okay they sure get in your way.

"Listen, Mel," Pop said when I had wolfed down every last crumb. "I've been thinking that if that Mr. Gilboa is such a good friend of yours he wouldn't mind meeting your parents, would he?"

"Christ, I'm no baby, Pop. How can I ask him that? I mean, how can I tell him, I can't see you or talk to you—"

"Or go with you to the races—"

"Yeah, the races and everything. How can I say I can't go unless Mom and Pop give you the onceover?"

"We can't have you going around with an older man we don't know."

"I can take care of myself."

Pop shook his head from one side to the other as if figuring out whether to agree or disagree. "I've got a lot of confidence in you, Mel. Ever since you could walk and talk you had something. Always landing on your feet. I remember once when Mom and you and me were walking on the boardwalk. You couldn't have been more than four or five.

And I don't know how it happened but we lost you. Maybe we stopped to talk to some friends and you disappeared." He went on to say how they were worried and looked everywhere and called the police, who checked all the lifesaving stations on the beach.

"Three hours later," he said, "do you remember where we found you?"

I wasn't sure I really remembered except that over the years they kept telling the story. "Sure," I said. "I was home asleep on the porch."

"Yep. You walked all the way through traffic and the summer crowds and found your way home by yourself. And when we asked you later what your address was, you didn't know. You just knew the way. Everybody thought it was a miracle. So you see, son, I knew even then that you could take care of yourself. But there are some things Mom and I want to be assured of. Like, for example, this man. We wouldn't want anything to happen to you."

I nodded. What else is there to do when your father talks like that? I mean, he didn't have a choice. Children can choose whether or not they love their parents. I think I love Pop. I even think I love Mom though she's a pain in the ass most times, wanting too much. As for Marcy, I could take or leave her.

"This man you see, this Mr. Gilboa—"

He stopped; he was very nervous suddenly. He wiped his nose with his handkerchief and didn't put it back in his pocket.

"This man—I'll tell you what worries us. You know there are older men who are sick. . . . They make friends with— you know, with young boys. . . ."

The sandwich and tomato juice jumped into my throat.

"You mean you think Franklin is a fruit, a fag, a *fagele*, a pansy?"

"You know all those words?"

"Christ, Pop, I'm in high school. I knew those words when I was a sixth-grader."

Heard them first when Eddie Norris, Sam Schwartz, and I used to sit on hot days in the shade under the boardwalk and show each other what we had. Once we were surprised by a tall thin grown-up guy with heavy eyebrows and a green Marine T-shirt who said he wanted to play games with us too. Quickly, without knowing exactly why, the three of us pulled up our pants and Sam, who was the oldest, yelled, "Get away, you homo!" The guy ducked out from under the boardwalk and scooted down the beach into a big crowd. I didn't know what a homo was.

Eddie was also innocent. "What's a homo?" he asked.

"A pansy, a *fagele*, a fruit," Sam said, showing off. I hated him for that.

"Sure," I said to Eddie. "Don't you know?"

"Nope. . . ."

"It's a guy who wants to fool around with kids," Sam said.

"You mean like we fool around?"

"Yeah," I said, jumping in ahead of Sam.

"So what's scary about it, if we do it?"

"Shit," Sam said. "You're a dope."

Eddie looked at me and I felt bad about his being called a dope. "He's younger than we are," I said.

"I'm not!" Eddie said.

"Okay, your father's a Hebrew teacher and that's why you don't know nothing," I said and felt satisfied.

By the time I was out of grammar school I knew all the words, and when I was with Marie Anderhorst down in the cellar or with my cousin Diana Levy in the bedroom when her folks and mine were playing bridge or canasta, I knew about boobs and getting a finger between the legs.

So I told Pop not to worry. Franklin wasn't like that. He was crazy about dames.

82

I waited for him to ask me if I'd gone all the way, but he didn't. Maybe he was too embarrassed. Mom would've whizzed the question to me like a fastball off Ted Williams' bat.

"I'm relieved," he said. "We try to teach you the right things, your mother and I, but I guess we can't hold a candle to the kids in the neighborhood." He touched my shoulder. "We come from an honorable family. My father was a rabbi in the old country. His father and grandfather before him. Good, honest people. Scholars too. I'm sure you'll never do anything that isn't honorable."

I wanted to take his hand and shake it like I was promising something. I mean, he really got to me. He couldn't help it if he didn't know I was different, that I could be anything I wanted to be, anything at all. I wished I could tell him what I was thinking, but that was going too far.

"I'll be as honorable as you are, Pop," I said, surprised at hearing myself say that but wanting to find something to please him.

Mom came in that minute. "Everything all right here?"

"He's okay, Anna," Pop said.

"What about that thing? Did you talk to him?"

"It's okay, Anna."

"Then what about girls?"

"Thank God, he likes girls."

"I like girls a lot, Mom," I said.

"You have no business liking girls at your age."

Pop came through. "It's never too early to begin."

I tell you if I had met Pop as a stranger, say sitting next to me at the track, I'd have really gone for him.

"Then when is this Mr. Gilboa coming to meet us?" Mom never let go.

"Let's leave it up to Melvin," Pop said.

I was feeling so good, so on top of things, full of pure bubble, that I had to open my trap and say, "I'll ask him."

With the look on Mom's face I knew right away I had made a mistake. But then I was sure Franklin wouldn't ever let me down.

9 The drug pushers were now moving into Harlem in a big way. Franklin, Hobie, Hayes, and a whole string of guys in the rackets were worried.

"Reason is simple," Franklin explained. "Money going into drugs is money that's *not* going into numbers. The take was down fifteen percent the last three months."

One day we were in Solly's Barbershop and Beauty Parlor with Hobie and Hayes getting their Madame Walker slicks. Franklin and I were in the book room, where the horsebook was. I was getting results on the phone and writing them on a blackboard. Early, there'd been a lot of talk about paying ten percent a week to Franklin's bankers for loans to settle some big losses.

"The pushers are keeping their prices low until the customers get hooked," Franklin was saying as Hobie walked in with his hair half slicked, half brushed up. Without his black glasses, I could see his eyes were small and close together.

"There's a dumdum out there, Franklin," he said. "Pickin' up a lotta trade. Want me to give 'em the boot?"

Franklin shook his head. He had told me once that Hobie was a killer with a short fuse.

"Is Cohalan around?" he asked, putting on his jacket.

"I looked through the window," Hobie said. "He's probably worryin' some poor bastard for havin' dirty headlights."

Franklin stuck a cigarette in his mouth and left. I put on

my jacket and followed. Hobie didn't say anything. And Hayes was asleep under a towel in the barber chair.

The pusher was a Puerto Rican, big and fat, and when we came out of the shop he was handing something to a colored girl with pokey braids down her back. I kept behind Franklin a couple of steps, wanting to see how he handled them. It was one of those muggy days when the sweat starts without your doing anything. At three o'clock in the afternoon the street was filled with kids and dames going shopping. One old dame with a walking stick stopped Franklin to say hello. He tipped his hat, said a few words, and bent down to kiss her old black cheeks. If you ever saw Cary Grant in the movies, you'd know what I mean when I say he moved like Cary Grant.

The pusher left the corner and walked up the street.

"Hey, Juan," Franklin called.

It was beautiful the way Franklin sounded. Sort of like calling a girlfriend you hadn't seen in a while. Loud enough to be heard, not too loud to scare her.

The pusher stopped, turned around, and waited for Franklin. He had a smile on his red lips that was stuck there like makeup.

"What you doing around here, *amigo?*" Franklin asked.

The pusher shrugged. "Free country, eh?"

"Sure. How about having a beer or two with me?"

"What for?"

"To talk a little."

"Hey, we ain't frien's."

"Could become friends."

The pusher began to shimmy a little, hopping on one foot and the other. I had seen only two guys smashed on horse or blue pills, and I think he was the third.

"Gotta go," he said.

"Come on, Juan, be a good fellow."

"Name's Carlos!"

"My mistake, Carlos."

Carlos turned to walk away. Franklin took his arm and brought him back.

"You're pushing in my territory," Franklin said.

"Fuck off!"

"Don't want pushers around."

"Ya hear' me, nigger."

I felt an explosion in the air, though the only noises came from the people walking by laughing and talking, the kids yelling and chasing each other.

"Cohalan's there!" I yelled to Franklin. I saw him coming out of a bar across the street. Suddenly I felt safe. I myself used to give Cohalan his weekly five bucks, plus ten for the sergeant and fifteen for the lieutenant.

"Cohalan!" Franklin called.

The cop waved his stick and kept walking away.

"Doc, get him. Tell him we got us a scumrunner."

I ran across the street, not caring about the cars.

"Franklin wants you," I said to the cop. "He's got a pusher."

His round Irish face was red, beer stink floating from it when he opened his mouth. "Tell him I got to get back to the stationhouse."

Suddenly Franklin was alongside. "What's holding you up, Barney? Build up your arrest record."

I looked across the street. The pusher was leaning against the wall, waiting. Which seemed very funny to me. Then the cop said, "I'm off duty, Franklin."

"What the hell does that mean? I'm giving you a pusher."

"It means I'm off duty."

Franklin grabbed Cohalan's buttons and pulled him to him. "What's the score, Barney? Damn it, what's up?"

"God be my witness, Franklin, my hands're tied."

Franklin let him go like he was a sack of garbage.

86

"It's organized now," the cop said, growling. "Big time. Mafia. Syndicate. Me. Horowitz. Riley. Who the hell knows? They're up to the captain and inspector."

"Christ almighty!" Franklin yelled, and everybody who was walking by stopped. "You're lettin' drugs come in. Openin' up Harlem to these sewer rats. You bastards!"

"Knock it off, boy."

"You fuckin' mick. When you go to mass next Sunday—"

"Shut up!"

"You'll drown babies in that shit! You'll bomb this town with shit! You'll sell your own fuckin' mothers for shit."

Cohalan raised his night stick. Franklin twisted away and backhanded the cop. Cohalan began to blubber. "What ya expect from a beat cop, fight Center Street?"

Some people came over to watch. Most of the others on the street, seeing a guy wrangling with a shamus, moved along quickly.

Franklin looked at Cohalan a long time. "I'm sorry for you," he said and walked back across the street. I don't think he even knew I was walking with him. Sweat dripped down his face and fell on a lapel of that great blue jacket he had on. I wanted to wipe it off but I thought I'd better not bother him then. He was away somewhere.

When we got to Solly's Barbershop and Beauty Parlor, Hobie was standing outside watching for us. Then suddenly this hopped-up pusher came around the corner and up to Franklin, yelling, "Get off my street, nigger!"

It was a long time before Franklin heard him. It was like one of those slow-motion movies. Then Franklin moved, sticking his leg between the pusher's legs, hooking him up to the crotch, and chopping him on the neck as he fell.

"Put it away, Hobie!"

I saw that Hobie had a .38 in his hand. He put it in his side pocket.

There was a big crowd all of a sudden. Women with shopping bags, men in bib overalls and workshirts, kids on skates, old grannies and hookers. They were all staring at the Puerto Rican, waiting to see what he was going to do.

Franklin pulled him up. The guy was shaking, almost falling. Franklin reached into the pusher's pockets and pulled out a few packets of the stuff and some loose red and blue pills.

"Throw this crap down the sewer," he said to me.

"My babies! My babies!" The pusher yelled like he'd been stabbed. He tried to break away from Franklin.

"These babies are garbage," Franklin said.

The pusher began to cry. "No! No! Me! My babies! At *casa*. Gotta pay for the stuff! How I pay? No money! No food!"

Someone yelled from the crowd. "Shove him down the sewer!" Others wanted to stomp him.

Franklin pushed the guy through the crowd, which broke open for him. "Beat it!" he said. The guy, still crying, ran down 115th Street like he was on fire.

"Poor eat poor like maggots on rotten meat," Franklin said to me when he came back. His eyes were bleary. When Hobie and Hayes, who had come out of the barbershop, tried to talk to him, he shook his head and walked away to the corner bar, Rosy's Cabin. I was damned unhappy, feeling sick.

Hobie and Hayes had to see their bankers, Venturi and Katz. They told me to go to Franklin. They didn't have to tell me.

I thought about things while I sat with him in the bar. Things like paying off cops, Franklin's craziness about drugs coming into Harlem, the policy business slowing down; like the way he sat in his chair, sopping up whisky, dead gone, like five inches had been cut out of the middle of his body. I didn't think anything could cut down Franklin Gilboa and I wanted to get up from my damned rum and coke and go to him, punch his shoulder or something silly like that, I mean, to show him that nothing was worth a damn. Or to reach over past the bottle of Cutty and take one of his cigarettes and start chewing it myself to get a grin on his caved-in face.

But I didn't do anything. I sat there, a lump on a plaster ceiling, making designs with beer spill on the table, half listening to the juke box working over Billie Holiday's "I Cover the Waterfront." Now and then I'd sneak a look at Franklin. He was sunk into the bottle. But the crazy part of it was that when he moved his glass or picked the next cigarette to chew, his hand was steady. Once we caught each other's eyes. He smiled, but there sure wasn't anything funny in the smile.

"Got to get out of the business," he said. "Can't compete with drugs, boy. . . ."

He went on talking and drinking, and all I did was keep saying yeah, yeah, wanting only to give him his play, to let the boiler boil.

"They swore on their mothers' lives they'd never do it. . . . Dogs. . . . Like everyone. . . . Follows the bitch's smell. . . . Hard cash and tremblin'. . . . World's full of it. . . . Fear and hard cash. . . . Never thought it'd hit me so hard. . . . I had my chicks, policy. . . . Hurtin' nobody. . . . Never thought. . . . I had this silver bullet. . . . Like you, Doc. . . . Never thought I'd lose it. . . ."

"Like me? Silver bullet? What's that?"

"With that silver bullet no witchdoctor'd get me. . . . I had smart bones. . . . Knew in my gut I could con the whole tribe. . . . Africa's the world, boy. Witchdoctors everywhere. Believe in witchdoctors?"

"No. . . ." I wished he'd tell me what he was talking about.

"I believe!"

Then he told me this nutsy story from a show he'd seen. About a black guy named Jones. Got out of a Georgia chain gang. Went to Africa. Conned a tribe into making him emperor. Got them to boil up some silver to make him a bullet. Told them nobody could touch him as long as he had that bullet.

Franklin was talking loud. Some guys from the bar moved over to listen. They knew Franklin and yelled to the boss to shut off the damned juke box.

They made a ring of faces and shining bar glasses as they moved closer. Franklin's voice came over like one of those Negro preachers I'd heard on the radio.

He told how this Jones had his enemies. "Guy with a crown on his head sooner or later gets a shiv up his ass. . . . Gotta keep your head down sometimes. Like we shoulda done behind the hedgerows in Normandy. . . . One day this Jones skedaddled to the coast to make his getaway with lots of loot. He had this pistol with five rounds plus the silver one. . . . But he got kinda rattled in his head and picked up this notion the boogers and witchdoctors were trackin' him. But he don't care. With that silver bullet they don't dare touch 'im."

He poured out some of the Cutty, spilling it on the table, and fingered his glass for a while.

"Tell it, man!" someone yelled.

"He don't care, at first. . . . But when he gets deep into a real black forest he gets nervous. . . . Hears noises, rattles. . . . Gettin' closer and closer. . . . He fires off his pistol. . . . Bang! Ain't no more rattles and noises. . . ."

"This a true story, Franklin?" a guy asked, shoving his big head into the light over the table.

"Forest got thicker 'n thicker. Moon went. . . . Got dark, wow! It got dark! . . . Like solitary in a Mississippi prison. . . . More noises aroun' 'im. Footsteps. Twigs breakin'. Old

Jones sure they're closin' in. Fires another shot. And another. . . ."

He took a deep slug and thought a while, then he went on, this time real quiet, to tell us how one by one the bullets got fired until Jones had only his silver one left.

"Didn't want to fire that one, did he? That was his luck, his life. Fire it and he gets blown out with it. But damn it all he hears those witchdoctor rattles. Sees shadows. Shivs and spears behind the trees. He's so scared he ain't thinkin' no more. Gotta save his life. So the poor bastard shoots off his last, his good one, the silver bullet."

There was a big "Ahhh" from the crowd. A sigh you could hear a mile away.

Nobody said anything. You could hear the clink of ice in a glass when a fellow put it down. Franklin had his head on his chest, his big arms on the table, the broken thumbs sticking out and throwing shadows. I don't know why but I was scared. Like I was Jones himself. Franklin said I had that silver bullet. Maybe that's what made me feel the way I always did. Could con the world. Like Franklin. Like Jones.

A squirmy little man with a shining bald head yelled, "Go on, man. What happened?"

"Shit, you know what happened. Without the silver bullet, he was mouse meat. They tore him apart."

"Who tore him?"

"The goddamn witchdoctors and their dumb kin."

"Oh, Jesus!" a man cried. Another moaned. My throat was sore and I couldn't swallow. Was Franklin telling us that he was Jones? I'd never believe it. Not even if he told me himself. He was in the dumps today, but tomorrow he'd be high again, struttin' along, patting the butts of the hookers and talking to the old folks.

Then he said that all of us think we're Jones. Got that bullet. Nobody going to hassle us. More than us. The whole

91

country. The old U.S. of A. thinks it's holding the silver bullet. Won a war. Chipper as a big buck after a good lay. No one's dropped bombs on Times Square. No Enola Gay let go a whap of atomic bombs over that wading pool in Washington. Right?

The crowd yelled, "Right!"

"Why? 'Cause God's on our side?"

"Hell, no!"

" 'Cause we're jus' too good? Too noble?"

"*Bull*-shit!"

"Tell it, man!"

"I'll tell you! This old U.S. of A.'s got the silver bullet. That's why! Whole damn country. No matter who's cheatin'. No matter what they do to niggers or the shit-poor whites. No matter what the dirty rich do! We got that silver-assed bullet."

The crowd kept yelling, "Yeah, man! Tell it! Jesus! Gospel truth!"

It was like a damn church. Even the bartender and boss and two drunks who could hardly stand joined in.

"But we ain't keepin' it forever," Franklin yelled.

They yelled back, "No, man!"

"We're going to fire the bullet someday. Like Greece and Rome and Babylon before. We're going to slide off the end of Coney Island."

Everybody was stamping their feet, clapping their hands, shouting, "Yeah, brother!"

I could smell the whisky and beer on their breaths.

"Nobody'll be left! Generals, presidents, all the soft pussy on the continent and all the cardjacks and flipper pricks. They'll all be done and gone."

Some yelled, "Holy! Holy!"

Franklin began to laugh, a wild nightmarish kind of laugh that stung like hot candle wax. People stopped chanting and yelling. It was scary.

He stood up from the table, knocking it over, glasses, booze, and everything. The skinny old man with the bald head would've fallen to the floor if someone hadn't caught him and held him up by the arms.

"But then someday," Franklin whispered, "someday a new kinda witchdoctor'll come along and he'll look aroun' and see nothin' but his close kin and maybe a skeleton or two. He'll get himself a nice clean hickory stick and start cuttin' a new story on it. And it'll start all over again. Yes, sir. It's all in the head. . . . And what else is there to livin' but tremblin' and hard cash?"

His body moved back and forth for a minute, his eyes staring at me like I was the silver bullet. "Don't you lose it!" he yelled, then bent a little and slid down on the floor, crashed and out.

We picked him up and put him on top of the bar to sleep it off. No one, not even the boss, said a word, and after a while guys had their drinks handed to them over Franklin's sleeping body.

I knew what he was telling me, that there wasn't a chance. He was hurting from the syndicate and Cohalan and a lot of that shit about people in business trusting each other like he told me the night we met. Maybe he was right and maybe he was wrong, but I'm a fast learner. I wasn't going to be any Jones. I wasn't going to stick my head up above the hedgerows. Before we slid off the end of Coney Island, I was going to have the bread, the chicks, the horses, and the cars, no matter how, legit or not legit.

I stayed at Franklin's side at the bar, wiping the sweat from his face, putting back his arms when they slipped over, making sure that he didn't fall off and that nobody bothered him. I waited until Hobie and Hayes came back. They said that Venturi and Katz would still bank them, but had raised the interest from ten to fifteen percent a week. I told them not to wake Franklin and we hung around, a kind of guard duty, until he opened his eyes, groaned, breathed in and out like he was running, jumped off the bar wide awake as ever, and asked me if he'd made a fool of himself.

"Hell, no!" I said.

Later I told him the folks wanted to meet him. He said sure, and when I warned him not to let on that I was running policy for him, he laughed and said, "Truth's like laying bricks. Just enough cement to hold them together, and not too much sticking out."

He made a date for Friday night. I should've known he'd do it. I didn't have to worry. We drove over to Em's. Vincy was free and we had a time that blew the top of my head off.

10 The day before Franklin was to come to the house, as I was leaving school I heard my name called. There was Hayes in his white hat and gold specs sitting in a shining red convertible Buick. I went over and he said, "I got word for you from Franklin. He can't make it to your place Friday night."

"What's up?"

"Nothin'. Just some business he's got to tend."

"Okay, but why couldn't he tell me himself?" I was worried. Nothing like this had ever happened before.

"He's busy, Doc. Just wanted me to let you know. You didn't expect him to call your folks, did you?"

"No. . . ." The thing sounded fishy. "Where can I call him? Em's?"

"Uh-uh. He's outta town for a time."

I didn't like that any better. Franklin would always let me know himself. "There's trouble, isn't there, Hayes?"

Hayes lit a cigar and shook his head.

"Come on, Hayes, tell me. Or I'll go into New York and look for him."

Hayes lifted his white felt hat, ran a hand over his slicked-down hair. It always got me nervous the way he did that. I don't understand why people have to use their hands one way or another when they think. Pull their noses. Diddle their chins. Make a big U with their lips. Scratch their cheeks. If you have to think, why can't you just think with your head?

"Franklin—" He started and stopped. "It'll have to be between you and me, kid. Cross your heart."

"I'm no baby, Hayes. I know how to keep a secret. Even if they break my thumbs."

"Okay. He's in the cooler. For assaultin' a citizen and resistin' Cohalan."

I felt like the sidewalk was moving and I hung on to the car. "What's going to happen?"

"They hung him with big bail. We're workin' on it now. Me and Hobie and Em."

"I got a couple hundred," I said. "We can go to the bank right now."

"It's after three, kid."

The whole thing was like something you heard on radio or saw in the movies. Like someone made it up. "How much is the bail?"

"Ten grand."

"Sell his car. Sell yours and Hobie's."

Hayes looked at me as if I were some nut from Bellevue. "What we get for 'em? Gumdrops. We're payin' on monthly."

"We got to do something!" I yelled, pounding my fist against the car until Hayes told me to stop. He said not to worry, they'd get Franklin's bail money before the day was over.

I worried the hell over it. I'm not good at losing anything, least of all Franklin, and my head felt like a football. I had to tell Mom that Mr. Gilboa was called out of town suddenly and would come to dinner some night soon.

Next afternoon right across the street from school, there he was in his car shining and grinning. I jumped in, my mouth split apart with my own big smile, but he didn't say anything about the arrest while he drove into Harlem. I was disappointed at first, but then I figured he was keeping it from me because he was proud and didn't want to let on that he hadn't enough juice to keep from being booked. When we got to Solly's Barbershop, Hayes and Hobie had more bad news. The cops were working an old racket to get money from pimps. Vincy had been picked up by a police car from another precinct while on her way to visit friends in Franklin's territory and had been taken to the station without being booked. One of the cops from there had called up to say that if they wanted the chick back they'd have to send someone over with a grand, otherwise they'd book her and she'd get a long, hot ride downtown. I was tied up in knots and all for moving fast.

"That's part of the same hassle on me," Franklin said.

"They don't know she's your chick," Hayes said.

"If they don't, why'd they call here?"

"Vincy told them, that's for sure," Hobie said. "You know Vincy. Them high-livin' whores at Em's can't belly the cooler. They go wild. Jee-sus, these days you need protection to spit. She told 'em to call here, Franklin."

Franklin said he smelled something bad. He could tell. But they had to spring Vincy. "Got the bread?"

"The day's take," Hayes said, pushing the gold-rimmed specs up on his nose.

"Let's get it to 'em fast," Franklin said.

"That makes eleven grand with your bail," Hobie said, the big money on his mind.

"So what? There'll be more comin'." Franklin was angry.

"Sure," Hayes said. "I checked Em. She's got Vincy lined up for a week's convention in Miami."

"Who'll take it?" Hobie said. "You can't, Franklin. Ya don't wanna be foolin' aroun' with bad cops. Work you over to make up for Cohalan. Or me and Hayes. They could get us on a vag and there'd be more bail money."

Franklin thought about it. I said I'd take the money but Franklin didn't jump. The other men said why not?

"I'll go," I said. "I'm not afraid. What could they do to me? I'll say someone I didn't know asked me to deliver a package." Franklin was still working on it. "It's okay," I said, really wanting to rescue Vincy. Like that guy Lancelot or whoever the hell it was in that poem Mr. Clothier gave us to read. It would make me feel good.

"Okay, Doc," Franklin said. "Tell it the way you said. A messenger boy. You don't know what's in the package or anything. And, for Chrissake, be careful."

I took a cab with the grand folded in an envelope—it was ten hundreds—and I wasn't afraid because Franklin wouldn't have agreed if there was real danger. Anyway, it was more like a dream than real. I was rescuing Vincy. The thought made me dizzy. I was in the cab but I was outside too, watching. And yet, dream or no dream, I could taste every breath of air that came into the cab and see things outside clearer than I ever saw them. The traffic, the people waiting to cross, the stores and buildings. It was as if I was riding through a street lit up by spotlights like at a Radio City Music Hall opening. The radios from the schlock shops on Lenox Avenue were loud and clear. I puzzled about it and then realized that it was like smoking a good stick of maryjane, a kind of high.

It was a rundown brownstone on East 95th near the river. The cop had said the grand was to be delivered to the basement door, ring one long, two short. I did. Nothing happened.

"Hey, kid, who you lookin' for?"

A white fellow with red hair was standing on the steps over me.

"Mr. Wolfe." That was the code.

"There ain't no Wolfe living there."

"Well, someone by that name said he wanted a package picked up."

"I'm the super and there ain't no such party. But try Fox on the second floor. 2B."

I went up the stoop. There was no one sitting there and that was a signal something was going on with cops. The hallway smelled of piss and I saw a dead rat against a wall. At 2B I knocked one long, two short. The door opened. A man with graying hair smoking a cigar waved to me to come in. The room was empty except for a phone. He held out a hand. I shook my head. Franklin said not to hand over the money until I saw Vincy. The guy went to the phone, dialed, and handed me the receiver. I heard Vincy's voice saying "Hello. . . ." I almost passed out.

"It's Doc. Where are you?"

There was a moment of silence. I was suddenly scared. "Where are you?"

A man came on. "Give him the bread and put him on."

"It's okay, Doc." That was Vincy again.

"Where are you?" I didn't know what else to say.

Again silence.

Holding the phone, I reached into my pocket for the envelope. It dropped to the floor. The man picked it up. He pulled out the notes, ran them through his fingers, and took the phone from me.

"Okay," he said and gave it back to me.

"Vincy!"

"Okay, Doc."

"Thank God!" My lips were shivering.

She hung up.

The man had left me alone. I walked to the door like someone who was told he was going to live after all. I'd never done anything as important as that before. God, I couldn't wait until Vincy and I were together again. Then, running down the stinking steps, I remembered that Hayes said she was going to a stupid convention in Miami for a week. I was ready to bawl like a baby, and I wasn't feeling so great anymore.

When I got back, Franklin had already spoken to Vincy and he congratulated me—the others had left—and gave me a free ride on a couple of numbers for the next day. On the way back to Beachport he made me tell him everything that happened. I'd done a damn good job, he said. He'd always known I had it in me. "Someday, Doc, you and I goin' to be legit, and you'll be runnin' a law office on Fifth Avenue. You hear, boy?"

I was still hanging on to Miami and I wasn't hearing anything else.

11 Mom, Pop, and Marcy waited in ambush for Franklin like a bunch of Indian braves. Pop wore a white shirt and a tie, Mom had spent the afternoon at the hairdresser's, and Marcy—well, Marcy looked like a billboard sign for Breck shampoo seen under a microscope. They tried to act as if they weren't excited, like it was nothing special having a colored man for chow. Hell, it didn't happen often, if ever, in the neighborhood. Even among NAACPers like Mom or the religious Socialists at Eddie Norris' house. Lots of big talk all around, but not much doing.

At exactly six-thirty the front doorbell rang. Franklin was wearing a black principal-at-graduation suit, and in his hands were some flowers for Mom and a bottle of Kosher-for-Passover Manischewitz wine. Wow! Even if it wasn't Passover.

I introduced Mom, Pop, and Marcy to Mr. Gilboa, who said to please call him Franklin, and that he was mighty happy to meet his friend's family. I'll be a sonuvabitch if he didn't speak in one of those phony Amos-and-Andy Southern accents.

They all said howdoyoudo and thanked him for the presents. Pop asked if he'd like a little whisky before dinner, but Franklin said that the wine with dinner would be jus' fine.

I got a real kick out of Marcy staring at him like she'd been hit in the head, and when he said later how much he felt at home and mentioned something a guy named Max Beerbohm wrote on the subject, I thought she'd fall over and faint.

Everything went nice and easy and so damned polite it was sick-making. Through dinner Pop explained about his business in insurance and Mom talked about her work getting petitions signed for the NAACP and the new Liberal Party. And how even as a girl at Wadleigh High School in Harlem she and her father had marched on behalf of the Scottsboro Boys. The way she talked you'd have thought she was the lady who threw the first tea into Boston Harbor.

They talked about the war and what happened to the Jews. Franklin said he had seen the concentration camps when he was with the Army in Europe, and there wasn't anything to say because no one's come up with the words to fit.

"Like seeing the pictures of Negroes lynched," Marcy said, putting her two cents in.

Pop changed the subject, saying that things were going to be different, but Marcy disagreed, claiming that there were people in the United States and England who wanted to go to war against Russia, and unless something was done, etc., etc.

After coffee, when we got back into the parlor and sat around in the easy chairs that nobody used unless there was company, Mom came on like a district attorney and asked Franklin what his business was. Boy, was I waiting for that!

"Ah understand what's behin' yore question, Mis' Henshel," he said, phony-baloneying it. "Yore son has spent some time with me, first at the pinball arcade, where we met, and then heah and theah. You-all are concerned, as I would be were he mah son. And Ah do have a son. Unfortunately, he lives with his mothah in Floridah. As parents, we sho' enough want to know their companions. Their character and interests. An' the fact that I'm a grown man, some years oldah than Melvin—" It didn't sound so bad when he said the name. "Why, of course, you-all would want to know about me."

He soft-soaped them like that for a while, and then he told them that after he left New York University during the Depression the best job he could get was running an elevator in an office building. Later he went to Florida and worked in a golf club as a waiter, until Pearl Harbor. He enlisted and was discharged in the summer of 1945, when he went to work at the arcade for a friend. In the year and a half since, he used his back pay and disability money—he'd been wounded in the Battle of the Bulge—to do a little investing here and there, real estate and so forth.

"Ah sure like to see pore folk put their hard-earned money where they can get a fair return. So Ah collect five heah, ten theah, and put it all together to buy this or that—a

101

barbershop, a bar, a tailor shop, horses to breed—and Ah'm proud to say that Ah've many satisfied clients as well as a few disgruntled ones when somethin' didn't come out as they expected. But then, sah—" He turned to Pop. "As an insurance man, you know the statistical tables."

"Certainly," Pop said.

Mom moved in. "Melvin says you take him to the track sometimes."

"Only when he tells me he doesn't have homework," Franklin explained. "The track, ma'am, is where we observe the improvement of the breed."

"He says he bets."

I broke in to say it was only once or twice.

"Ah believe, ma'am, that bettin' at the track, mind you, where it's legal, done moderately, is a great teacher. It teaches us the value of money. A dollar earned with sweat when it's thrown away bettin' makes us value that dollar more. And if yore horse happens to come in, you fin' out that easy-won money goes away jus' as fast. Ah appreciate that some folks lose their rent and food money. That's bad. Real tragic. And when they suffer for it, they learn what's important and what isn't."

He reached over to lay off the ash from a cigar Pop had given him.

"Then theah's the beauty of it. Horses, even standin' still, are fine things to look at. And when they're in motion—" He sighed. "Like breaking waves on the beach." He turned to Marcy. "Mis' Marcy, do you know that poem about horses, written, Ah believe, by Lord Byron?"

Marcy blushed and said that she didn't know it but would look it up. Franklin apologized for not being sure it was by this Byron fellow, perhaps earlier or later.

Mom charged in again. "But where does Melvin get the money to bet? I found a hundred dollars under his bed."

Franklin looked at me as if I had spit on the carpet. I mean, sad and disgusted at the same time.

"You didn't tell them," he asked me softlike, "that what you won at the pinball machines Ah paid you in cash?"

"That's right. And I used that money to bet on a long-shot at Jamaica. . . . I told ya all that, Mom!"

Franklin turned and waved his arms like a lawyer who'd just won a case. "Theah it is, ma'am."

"I don't want my son to go to the races anymore," Mom said. "I'm opposed to betting in any form. It takes money from the poor and gives it to racketeers. One of the great evils of capitalism. And, if you don't mind my saying so, Mr. Gilboa, I can't understand why you'd want to waste your time on a snotnose kid who should be studying instead of betting on horses or learning how to drive a car or whatever else you do together. People tell me that you did funny things at your shoeshine stand last summer. Numbers, is it?"

I thought Marcy would bite Mom because of the way she was talking to Franklin. As for Pop, he half got out of his chair, then sat down and up and down like he had a pain in the behind. "Look, Anna, I go to the races and bet my two dollars, don't I?"

I was angry too, but I was also wondering how Franklin was going to handle Mom. He lit his cigar, even though it didn't need it. Like I told you once, he always took time to think.

"Ma'am, Ah don't min' at all yore sayin' what you did. You-all have the best reason in the world to question mah friendship with yore son. Well, Ah'll be pleased to explain. As Ah said before, Ah have a son too. But, as you-all might say, he's lost to me. By that Ah mean his mothah and Ah are separated. An' she done a bad thing. Turned him against me. Well, it's a great loss for a man to lose his son. Isn't that right, Mr. Henshel?"

Pop moved his head up and down like a yo-yo. I looked at Mom. The only thing on her face was Mr. District Attorney.

"Ah took a likin' to young Melvin because Ah saw that he was a good boy, a real good boy, who respected his elders—" Marcy opened her mouth to say something but changed her mind. "Ah saw he was ambitious to make somethin' of himself. Maybe not exac'ly what you have in mind, but Ah could tell that sooner or later he'd grow up to understan' the value of school and college. And maybe even law school. Yes, ma'am. You can understand that boys'll tell others what they'll nevah tell their own folks. Why many a time he'd say to me, 'Franklin, Ah want to be a judge someday.' That's right, Ah thought. We could all use an honest judge comin' from fine upstandin' folk with real American values."

He cleared his throat and flicked the ash off his cigar, then smiled. "An' in truth, ma'am, if Ah was his confidant, he was mine. Ah could tell him about mah son and how Ah missed him, and how he could help me feel there was someone young who'd think well and good of me. Ah needed him. You-all wouldn't want him goin' off with a bunch of loony kids pickin' wrong companions and learnin' wrong things."

He talked on like that and I tried to keep a serious look on my face. Christ, he was a wiz. Marcy couldn't get over it; she kept shifting her head from Franklin to me and back again like she was watching a tennis game. Pop was in Franklin's hand, but Mom was still holding out.

"Howevah, if you-all feel Ah'm takin' advantage, please tell me an' Ah won't see the lad anymore. That is, if you-all feel you can't share yore son with another man who's lost his."

A minute later he stood up and said politely that he thought it best to leave and let the folks talk about what would be right without his being there.

"Ah sure appreciate this chance to meet you-all," he said.

"And Ah enjoyed every morsel of that marvelous dinner."
He shook hands with Pop, who said that he hoped he'd
come again.

Marcy was on her feet too and shook hands. She was still
too stunned to say anything except that she'd look up the
Byron poem and send a copy to him through me.

"Mis' Marcy," Franklin said, "Ah'd appreciate that, yes,
Ah would. But may Ah add a pussonal note? Melvin heah
speaks of you a lot and he really likes you. But like the rest
of us human folk, he needs all the understandin' we can
give 'im."

I almost died listening to him work over my sister. She
was taking it all in, moving her head up and down like a
child being asked if she wanted to go to the circus. More
than that, she had fallen for Franklin so hard that her tits
were standing at attention.

"Now Ah do know, Mis' Marcy, that children don't always
get on real happy with each othah, and Ah been meanin' to
talk to Melvin heah about the respect that young-uns got to
give the older ones. Ah know he's got a funny way of showin'
his likes and dislikes. But real deep down he thinks the
world and all of his sister." He turned to me. "Now, don't
ya, Melvin? Speak right up and say what you always say to
me."

I could've kicked him in the hot place and wanted to yell
something dirty, but I saw Pop and Mom looking at me
hard, and then Marcy too, so I tried to find something to say
that wouldn't make me throw up Mom's food. I worked my
throat over a couple of times with an uh and ah and some
coughing. Then Marcy broke in.

"I know what you're talking about, Mr. Gilboa, and it was
kind of you. Very kind. But unnecessary. I know that Mel
loves me. As you say, it's just his manner. Right now he's a
crazy kid, but you and I know he'll grow out of it."

"Exac'ly, Mis' Marcy," Franklin said, not looking at me at all.

Mom was the last to shake hands. "I'm glad you think that Melvin is a good boy, but to be honest I still feel that it is best for him to have friends his own age."

"Ah hope, ma'am, that the fact of my being colored has nothin' to do with it."

"God, no!" Mom said, almost shouting. "We're not prejudiced people. Some of my best friends are colored."

"Ah'm glad to hear that," he said and walked to the door, with Pop and Marcy trailing behind like a couple of trained dachshunds.

"I'll take you to your car," I said and ran out ahead of him.

At the car he said, "How'd I do, Doc?"

"You're the greatest! You had them eating out of your pocket."

"Your Mom's a tough biddy."

I could have given him odds on that.

"And I don't think her chicken soup and roast beef's worth a damn."

That was okay with me too.

"That cornball accent gets them every time," he said. "Genteel. Mint juleps. Scarlett O'Hara and all that shit."

"Talking about that," I said, "where'd you get that poetry *schtick?*"

He leaned into the front seat of his car and pulled out a book. "Bought it yesterday. *The Reader's Companion*. Got everything in it." He slapped my back and grinned. "Ah believe, sah, in bein' *pre*-pared! Which reminds me, how come you didn't have sense enough not to hide money under a bed? Don't you know that's the first place house burglars look? And suspicious wives? And mothers?"

"She never cleans under my bed. We got this colored

woman coming in once a week. She must've been sick the last time. Besides, where the hell else could I keep it?"

"In a bank."

"You told me money's for spending."

"Under a bed?"

"It was dumb. But I told them I was going to buy birthday presents with it."

"Play it cool now, boy. Don't want your folks throwing you out."

He asked me to call him at Em's the next day after school and drove off. I went back upstairs like I was walking into Sing Sing's death row.

There's no point in going into the whole mess. Marcy said that Franklin was the most charming and literate man she'd ever met and she couldn't make out what he saw in me. Mom said he was a great *schmeichler,* which means a talker who smiles and gets away with telling people what they want to hear. But that didn't change her mind. She and Pop decided that I could see Franklin no more than once a week and then I had to tell them where I was going. I looked at Pop. "Until you're older," he said. "It's better this way."

I didn't argue. Be cool, Franklin said. It just meant I'd have to lie a little more.

12 Not even my birthday helped. I was going crazy. Pop made his usual speech about how I was born during the Depression and how he hoped when I grew up there'd be no more unemployment and anti-semitism like Hitler's. He gave me a white knockabout jacket. He also said he was sure I'd be a good Jew, but I didn't know what the hell he was talking about, since the only Jewish stuff I knew was chicken on Friday night and Pop going to temple on Yom Kippur. Mom gave me a cashmere pullover and a subscription to some magazine called *The Nation*. Jee-sus! It didn't even have a sports column. Marcy's present was, as the comic said on the Fred Allen show, underwhelming. A book! Of poetry! Walt Whitman! Which I had enough of, thank you, in Mr. Clothier's English class.

Franklin put ten bucks on a triple combination in my name which didn't come in. Vincy said she canceled a john to spend an hour with me as a happy birthday, but we got into a fight anyway about her being too busy the week before.

By the time the baseball season started, it was worse. How do you figure it? I had more money than ever in my whole life—$597.83 in the Dry Dock Savings Bank. I won a long shot, and Franklin gave me a one-percent interest in a body shop he bought with Hobie and Hayes in Brooklyn near where all those nutsy Jews with their long beards and hair curling over their ears lived. Marcy was laying off her wisecracks because she won a scholarship and was applying for a transfer to Wellesley.

I didn't have to lie more than twice a week to Mom when she asked me if I was seeing Franklin. And Eddie Norris and I stopped speaking after he said he would no longer help me do the essays for Mr. Clothier's English class.

The fact is I was going batty. I couldn't sleep. I wasn't even sure I wanted to live through it. The dogs running on the beach were happier than I was. What I'm trying to say is that Vincy was driving me up the wall.

It wasn't exactly her fault. She was trying her best to slow me down. I was the one who was socking it into myself. But I couldn't let her go. I wrote her stupid letters which I didn't mail. I took cold showers twice a day, even when it wasn't warm enough outside to sweat. I hung around Em's whenever I could, but Em said I was getting in the way. So I used to hide near the entrance of the apartment house on Central Park West, and when I saw Vincy come out with one of her johns I'd try to talk to her. She wouldn't talk to me—except once when she swore that she'd tell Franklin if I didn't lay off hustling her.

But that didn't stop me either. The next time I came prepared. I took fifty dollars out of my savings bank and when she came down the elevator—I was standing behind it on the ground floor and could see her through the grill— with a john talking in some kind of foreign accent, I followed them. She was wearing that gray silk dress Franklin bought for her at Saks Fifth Avenue one day when I was with them. She looked like Grace Kelly. So damned beautiful and re- spectable.

The john was saying, "Yes, my darleeng, I am ze man who was in ze picture with ze Aga Khan." They moved to a Bentley. Vincy said, "I never drove a car like that. Could I try?" He said yes, and they both got in. I went down the street behind them, picked up a cab, and told the driver to follow the car.

"Ya got the dough, kid?" he asked.

"More than you made today, buster," I said, hating his guts. "Let 'er rip."

I didn't know what the hell I was doing. I wasn't playing any silly movie detective, you know, pretending that I was Humphrey Bogart. No, I was me, Doc Henshel, and if I didn't know what I was doing I knew that I had to do it, like sneezing or blinking your eyes.

The Bentley went into the park toward Fifth Avenue.

"How close ya want me to get to him?" the hackie asked.

"I don't care. Just don't lose him."

"Don' want no trouble."

"Christ, who's asking you to ram him or something? I just want to know where they're going, that's all."

"It could run ya into money."

I dug into my pocket and came up with a twenty, a ten, and a couple of ones. I shoved the twenty in front of me. "Satisfied?"

The Bentley didn't leave the park. It went uptown to 110th Street then back toward 59th. As long as Vincy was driving, I wasn't feeling so bad. It was a nice sunny day. Maybe they were just going for a run around the park. At around 72nd the car stopped at a red light. We were two cars behind them but it was at a curve and I could see them. Suddenly Vincy and the john got out and changed seats. Now he was driving. That sure buzzed me because they'd be going somewhere, his place or hers. It gave me a little time to think. What the hell could I do if I saw where they went? I didn't want to show myself. That would be nuts and it would make me feel lousy to let on that I was following them. But I wanted to see them together going in some- where. That may sound crazy, because you'd think that was the last thing I wanted to see. But, damn it, it wasn't. Just the opposite. Like hating castor oil and drinking it to get rid of the cement in the gut. When they got out in front of the Sherry-Netherland Hotel and entered, I drank the castor oil okay but the cement in the gut was even heavier.

I didn't get much change for my twenty, just enough for a big tip to show the crummy hackie that I was no kid, and then, because I couldn't help it, I sat in the lobby of the hotel watching the elevators and eating Hershey bars I bought at the drugstore. Not wanting to miss Vincy, I couldn't go to the can for anything, and believe me that was rough.

Usually, I didn't mind watching people, and there were all these characters checking in, checking out, all so damned important, movie people maybe and rich chicks with their furs and dogs. After a while they all looked alike except one dame. I was sure I knew her from somewhere. Some brass-assed guy with a flower in his lapel met her halfway through the lobby and said in a voice that could carry from Canarsie to Hoboken, "Welcome, Miss Dietrich!" In a way I was disappointed at how she looked, so I ripped open another Hershey and chewed without tasting it much.

I told myself not to think of what was going on upstairs. I would pick out some dame and undress her in my mind but it didn't help. As soon as I got her coat off, I'd be there with Vincy and that john, in bed and all that.

The whole thing made me feel like my skin was suddenly covered with scabs or rat bites. I wanted to get a drink of something, take the taste of the damn Hersheys out of my mouth, but I was afraid I'd miss her.

I tried to think of things. Once when I was maybe eleven or twelve me, Eddie Norris, and a pug-nosed redhead called Hartzy, who was older, were hanging around Goldberg's soda fountain. A new girl, really a slicknick chick, was dishing out the goodies.

Hartzy said to us, "Watch this." He went to the counter and said, "Hey, kiddo, let's have a virgin coke."

"What's a virgin coke?" she asked.

"One with a cherry in!"

That was terrific. God, how we laughed, even though I wasn't sure what he meant. The doll didn't like it. She ducked her head and squirted some coke in the glass like she was upset.

"Hold it," Hartzy said. "Fuck the coke. Make it plain."

This time the girl dropped the glass and the coke spilled on her dress. Goldberg came running over from the pre-scription department yelling, "Vat gives here?" He was one of the German refugees, a nice old gent, who got out in time, according to Mom, and I sometimes think by the way she sounded that she never forgave him for it.

"They're talkin' dirty, Mr. Goldberg," the girl said, beginning to cry.

"Vat they say?" he asked, then changed his mind. "Vorget it." He turned on me and Eddie Norris. "I know your volks, young man. You vant me maybe to tell them?"

I was feeling lousy because the girl was crying and maybe she'd have to pay for the coke and the broken glass. I always feel that way when characters get kicked around when it isn't their fault.

"I'm sorry, mister," I said. And Eddie said the same. "It wasn't her fault," I added and stuck a dime on the counter.

Outside, Hartzy called me a *schmuck*, and I would have kicked him in the ballocks but Eddie grabbed my arm. "He's bigger'n you," he said. Hartzy could have knocked my head off if he'd tried, so I said, "Sticks and stones can break my bones, but names'll never hurt me." And me and Eddie ran away.

I couldn't think of anything else while Vincy was banging the john upstairs. I took another Hershey but it stuck in my throat and I had to spit it out into one of the plants when no one was looking.

I couldn't hold my pee in anymore, so I ran down the stairs to the Men's, did what I did, and clumped back up the stairs three steps at a time. When I got back to the lobby an old lady with a dog on her lap had taken my chair and I had to stand around trying to make out I was important. I wasn't sure Vincy was still upstairs but I decided to wait another hour in case it wasn't one of those all-night tricks. My legs were hurting bad and I walked up and down from the front door to the elevators to get the cramps out. I was going to be late for dinner and I began working on what lie I would tell the folks when I saw Vincy crossing the lobby toward a row of telephone booths. Forgetting everything I was going to do, I ran to her like a lost kid, yelling, "Vincy!"

She turned around. I thought she didn't know who I was. Then she said, "What the hell are you doing here?" I couldn't tell whether she was angry or not. All I knew was that I wanted to put my arms around her and kiss her.

"I was paying off a guy for Franklin," I lied. "One of the bell captains."

Suddenly I didn't want to kiss her; I wanted to hit her, to get even.

"Did you get boffed good?" I said, tasting the sour stuff in my throat.

Her blue eyes squinted and she hiked the fur scarf around her throat like she was feeling a cold wind off the Hudson. "How'd you know I was here?"

"I knew! I knew!"

"You followed me here," she said, disgusted, and left me to go to the phones. I waited, then followed her.

She was speaking to Em, asking if she had a date waiting, and then if Franklin was there. He wasn't. She hung up and looked at me as if I was crazy.

"You're crazy," she said.

"I love you. . . ."

"You shouldn't have followed me. Franklin'll give you hell."

"You won't tell him."

Some fat dame walked between us with a nasty look at Vincy.

"What're you looking at?" I said to the dame.

Vincy shut me up and said, "You look ready to faint. Let's go for a drink."

We went into the bar next door, where the stupid waitress asked if I was old enough for the Cutty Sark I ordered. I said I was going to be a grandfather any day and she winked at

Vincy, who had ordered a gin fizz, and brought me a coke. Vincy told me not to argue and gave me a sip of her drink.

Then she began to explain to me how she was a professional at her job and she didn't want to get involved with anyone on a love basis. "I understand how you feel, Doc, but it won't work. I already told you that."

I saw suddenly that her lipstick was crooked over one edge of her mouth. "We're great when we're together. But that doesn't mean I'm going to knock off and be a singleton for one guy. Not for little ol' Vincy Bogart. You're Dapper Dan in the sack, honey, but that's all it's going to be."

I wanted to reach over with a finger to wipe the lipstick clean, and then I thought it was funny how when she was with me she ditched all her lady-type talk. Didn't that prove she was closer to me than to any john? But I couldn't tell her that. All I could say was that I hurt. But that didn't get to her. She talked tougher and tougher and I got real angry and lost my head. I knocked over the glass on the table and told her she was a lousy lay. Everyone in the bar stopped to look. A guy came over and asked Vincy if I was being obnoxious. Goddamn right I was. I was so friggin' obnoxious I could've bit my tongue off for saying what I did and thrown her the pieces. Instead I stood there trembling and heard her say real calm, "It's all right, sir. He's just a friend and a little drunk." She threw some dough on the table and walked out. I went after her, and she told me to leave her alone, she never wanted to see me again.

"I'm not going to leave you alone. I love you!"

People were slowing down near us, but I didn't care. I felt like an empty barrel rolling down a hill. She walked toward 59th Street. I followed. The crowds coming and going were all around us and I was afraid I'd lose her so I ran up and grabbed her arm.

"Knock it off, Doc. You'll get cops comin' over an' askin' questions."

I thought I'd try another angle. "You really never want to see me again?" I worked hard to sound sincere and told her that I'd walk away if she said so.

"You got it right, boy," she said and went to the curb to hail a cab.

One had just emptied and she opened the door. I felt like a piece of garbage the tide had slapped down on the beach. Suddenly everything hurt, my legs, my shoulders, my fists.

She leaned forward to talk to the cabbie, a smudge of gray silk dress behind the dirty window. The cab didn't move. There was a lot of traffic ahead and behind it. Everybody blowing horns, the way it was the day the war ended and Pop took me to Times Square to see the crowds and I watched the sailors and soldiers drinking out of bottles and kissing the girls.

I stared at Vincy through the cab window. People shoved me one way and another. Traffic cops whistled, guys and dames stuck their heads out of cars, yelling. Crosstown buses growled again. I saw the gray dress move. The door opened like in a dream.

"Doc!"

In all the noise I was sure I heard it. But it still could've been a dream.

"Come on! Hurry!"

I floated past a bunch of school kids with their books, past dames with packages. In the dream I was lifted inside. I smelled Vincy's perfume. I saw the smear of lipstick. I felt her hand pulling me down to the seat next to her.

"You're a crazy sonuvabitch, Doc. And I'm as nuts as you are. But I'll kill you if you tell Franklin."

She kissed me and put my hand on the gray dress over her breast. Slowly, the traffic got loose and we moved.

115

When I came out of the dream and felt her hand pressing mine, I knew I had her again and good.

13 Toward the end of the spring term Mr. Clothier, my English teacher, called me into his office to tell me the great news that unless a miracle happened I was going to flunk English and history and would have to repeat them in summer school. I did what I could to look sad but that didn't seem to get to him, although he was a nice enough Joe who wore loud ties, patches on his jacket elbows, and a wild silk handkerchief in his breast pocket. He never pressed too hard but he made you feel that he should be getting good things from you. For someone like me, who wasn't interested in anything like Chaucer or Shelley or Whitman, all his favorites, there wasn't much good to give. But I sure didn't want to go to summer school, and as for dropping out I wouldn't get very far with Franklin or for that matter the folks. I was up the creek and I had to get me a paddle, so I said with my poor-boy voice that there were problems in the family that probably got in the way of my studying.

"What kind of problems?" Mr. Clothier asked, as ready to help as a Boy Scout with a blind old lady.

That was a lousy question. "I'd rather not say, sir."

"But my job is to be useful in such cases. After all, we shouldn't be asking more than a student can do, considering special circumstances."

"That's fine, Mr. Clothier. But I promise I'll do my best to catch up. I really will. I'll take care of that problem, sir."

He looked disappointed as hell. "Well, Henshel, if you don't want to confide in me, I can't force you, of course."

"Yes, sir."

"If it's a divorce in the family—"

"Oh, no, sir!" I stood up and headed for the door.

"Alcoholism can be treated by one of any number of methods."

"It's not that, sir." Why the hell had I brought the family in?

"Things are pretty tough economically in this postwar period, and if your family's in any trouble—"

"My father's got a good job, sir."

"Then what in God's name is it, Henshel?"

I was thinking hard.

"If anything affects your study habits or your attention in class, it must be important. To you—and to me. You're not a stupid boy. You've got a lot of possibilities. I remember your class report on Romeo and Juliet. It obviously interested you. It had real quality. What's wrong, Henshel?"

What's wrong? Could I have told him that Eddie Norris wrote that report for me? (Eddie said it was the last time he would do my work. It was unethical, he said. I called him a Judas and he said if he was Judas that would make me Jesus, and that was going too far.)

"I don't know, Mr. Clothier." I edged toward the door. "I'll do better. You watch and see." I beat it down the hall, out of the side door, and scrammed to pick up the *News* to get the word about the day's race results.

14 One Saturday when I was driving with Franklin to watch Citation run with Eddie Arcaro up in the Belmont Stakes, I could tell he was worried by the way he held the wheel and cut off cars trying to get into his lane. Usually he was full of juice going to the races, talking horses and jockeys and telling me what to watch for, because he believed by this time that I was going to have horses of my own someday. I was sorry for him because I was floating. Vincy and I had been together twice that week, and I was hoping he didn't know.

The radio was turned on to the news. Truman had made a speech about the Republicans and there was some kind of fighting in Palestine.

"I got a call from your mother," he said, turning it off.

"You did?"

"I did!" He sounded nasty.

"Uh-uh. . . ."

"She told me you were doing rotten in school."

"Shee-it, Franklin, she's always griping."

"You got a bad report card."

"Not in math I didn't."

"History, English, French. You're flunking."

"Not phys. ed."

"You been playing hooky. They sent for her."

I'd had that out with her and Pop. I claimed the attendance records were all wrong, and I tried that on Franklin.

"You're lying to me, Doc."

I didn't say anything.

"I told you about lying to me," he said, punching the horn at a passing garbage truck and shooting past it.

I said I was sorry, but I don't think I got anywhere. But then he laid off me and began to spill out a lot of stuff about how he hated Cohalan and the Biggies behind him all the way up to the top. They were worse than the Commies. Cancer. Not getting it up. A-bomb. I was scared by the way he sounded, not that I ever thought he couldn't hate people if they were shits, guys who double-crossed other guys, snitchers who worked for the cops, dames who got way out of line, welshers like Till, and so on. But the way he spit out the words, choking the wheel with his hands and playing chicken with traffic, I knew, just as I knew before, that Cohalan had gotten under his skin, had made him crawl, had cut his balls off.

Then he started on me as if it was all part of the same gripe. Who did I think I was? Why was he wasting time on me? Didn't I know that he was counting on me? When I got through college and went to law school, it would be through me that he'd go legit. Sure, it would take time. But he would need that time to put aside enough seed money to set me up and invest through me in bars, horses, automobile agencies.

"Sooner or later the whole country's going to be in the pushers' pockets. But not me. Not Franklin Gilboa. Not you either. You're my silver bullet!"

God, I didn't know what to say or feel or anything but to keep holding on to myself. Who was I? Before meeting Franklin I was Pop and Mom's bad boy. The three of clubs to Marcy's queen. A pest. A slob. A pain in the ass. They keep saying it's home sweet home. Bull! It's a roof. Food. Bed. And a lot of nagging until I didn't know who I was. That's not true. I knew. I was a big *disappointment*. Now Franklin was telling me again he needed me. Wow! I had to be told again and again. Got my gun. Here come Carlson's Raiders. Gung ho! Randolph Scott and all that! *Franklin needs me!*

Then he was telling me something else. His girls did what he told them to do or he kicked them out of Em's. Let them crawl the streets. He'd taught them, given them a cushy run, soft tricks, no overwork, a fair cut on the take, pretty clothes, beauty treatments, a chance to meet the bright rich guys. But he didn't want them to count on him to coddle, love, warm their tootsies on a cold night. He was Mr. Gilboa and they were—whoever the hell they were. Just as he wouldn't kiss ass with the drug syndicate that was blasting his turf, making junkies who didn't produce anything worth a shit—so he wouldn't kiss ass with anyone. And that meant anyone. (Was he talking about me?) He'd go just so far for partners. Loyalty, yes, when it came to protecting anyone from the cops. But if there was too much rubbing around, too much taking, too much cutting into him, then that was a dead end. "Feeling good, bad, angry, sore, happy, up, down, and sideways, it's okay with me, Doc. But feelings that get too close to what a man is for himself, no!"

Then he shut up and turned on the radio low to a jazz station, and we didn't say anything while he drove in and out of traffic like a drunk. There was something boiling there.

"You been seeing a lot of Vincy," he said suddenly, and I knew I was on the griddle.

"I love her," I said, feeling honest saying it. And not afraid. He needed me, didn't he?

"You're not going to see her anymore. I put out the word."

"No!"

"Vincy isn't going to see you."

"You can't do that!"

"You asking to get her kicked out into the street?"

I wanted to cry but I didn't, not exactly.

He pulled into a side street, turned off the motor, and shoved himself around the seat until he faced me. He gave me one of his handkerchiefs. "You want to cry, cry!"

"I love her," I mumbled.

"Fuck that."

"I don't care!"

"Tell me what this love business is about."

"You never been in love?"

"You tell me what it's like."

120

"I don't know. . . . You want! That's all. . . . Yeah, you want! You want her. You try getting laid with someone else but either you can't get it up or it don't mean anything. . . . Everything with her is great, her looks, her smell, when she talks, laughs, screams. . . . You want every square inch of what she's got. . . . Everything she is, she has. . . . And it isn't all pussy and tits. Hell, no. When that's over with, I want more. . . . Her. . . . It. . . . Whatever the hell she has! I want! When I don't see her for a day, when she's not there, at Em's, I want to go stick my head in the can and flush it down. I try to think of something else but I can't. I sit in school like a dummy. I can't blow her away. Nothing she does or has turns me off. Nothing. I want it all! And when I think of her with the johns, I go potty, loopy, nuts, dango and down! A bad dream. . . . So bad I want to kill her!"

"Got a gun, have you?"

"No. . . ."

"But if you had you'd kill her?"

"No. . . . I just think about it."

"And I suppose when she's at Em's with some john, you feel—"

"Like spit on a wall," I said.

"Do you wait until they go out together and run down the stairs hoping you'll get to the street before they drive off so you can follow them?"

I was knocked out. "Who told you? How do you know?"

"You got the greens. You been pussy-whipped. It's an old street, chum. A very old one. But at each end is a high brick wall like one of the concentration camps I saw in Germany. You walk that street and you're in prison. You got to learn. I warned you before."

"Nothing you say'll keep me away from her," I said. "Even if you throw her out, I'll find her."

"She's not going to thank you."

"You don't know. . . . You don't know!"

He shook his head like an angry punch-drunk prizefighter. "A pile of nothing, that's what you'll be! And don't give me that crap about it being more than ass. You don't know what love is. All you know is what your prick tells you. And, boy, that's like a traffic light. Red, stop. Green, go. It's what keeps us moving. Sure, it's the key to the world, but you never know what door you open. On the other side could be anything, a good lay or a lady friend ready with a shiv. Or you could get laughed at with your pants down your legs and nowhere to go. You think it's the greatest thing since coca-cola. And it is. You think you got God almighty between your legs, and you have. But, boy, you also got a .38 that could rip your guts to pieces. Get it in! That's all you think about. But it's a dark forest there, like where they cut Jones to pieces." He took a long breath and wiped his forehead. He was angry and rubbed the sweat from his hands and looked down at his broken thumbs.

"You got to have control. For everything. Mostly yourself. Or else you're not free. I tell you, if you let dames get into you instead of you getting into 'em—if you don't learn to say bye-bye baby, it's been nice and maybe I'll see you next week—I tell you, the fucking you get's not worth the fucking you get. Keep your cock hard and your heart cool. And that goes for everything!"

I said something I never dared say to Franklin. "Bullshit!"

He leaned over and slapped my face hard. I reached over to hit him back, but he held my arm until it hurt too much and I begged him to let go.

"You want to fire your silver bullet so soon?" he said. "Let the witchdoctors get to you? Well, boy, I'm not going to let them! I'm going to help you keep that bullet if I have to cold-turkey you."

I didn't know what he meant and I didn't care.

Citation won the Belmont that day and paid $2.20, which was nothing for the bettors. But he looked beautiful, ran the mile and a half easily, his great head high and mighty. I could've kissed him when he stood there getting the flowers. I swore that someday I'd be in that winner's circle with my hand rubbing the light sweat off my horse's rump, giving orders to cool him gently.

"Racehorses," Franklin said, "are better than the best women. It's okay to love them."

15 It was final-exam time and I had to study if I was going to keep out of summer school. I worked out a deal with Eddie Norris to help me with my back assignments by promising to help him go through the neighborhood to collect money for some crazy club called Youth Zionists. He and his family were hot and bothered about Israel, which was okay with me, but I told him there also ought to be a Youth for Colored People. I gave him the dope on some of the things I'd heard around Harlem and what went on in the South. Did he know that colored people couldn't sit downstairs in Southern movie theaters? Or that they couldn't use the same crapper and drinking fountains as whites? Or that they got hanged on trees or tarred and feathered if they spoke up for their rights?

"We're for the colored too," he said.

"They got them in Israel?"

"No. Here."

"Then why you collecting for them?"

"Because they're Jews and we're Jews."

He gave me some cockamamie story which I didn't understand and I told him I was for anybody who was being hustled. (Just between you and me, I'd have collected dough for Eskimo bears to get his help for the exams, so I agreed to the deal.)

I called Franklin to say that I wouldn't be around for a while but there was no answer at Eppie's or his pad on Fifth Avenue and 95th Street. (The Beachport one was locked up.) I called Em like he told me to do if he wasn't around at the places but she said he was busy. The *Daily News* hadn't run any stories on a policy raid in Franklin's territory so I didn't think it was that. God, a whole week went by, and I missed him. I was real worried. Thinking of the Biggies. And with all the studying crap, I didn't have time to see Vincy but once.

Then one day as I finished my last final exam in Mr. Clothier's class with some damn fine crib notes I'd worked up without letting Eddie Norris know, I scooted out of school and saw Franklin in his Caddie across the street. I ran to him through the traffic like a Green Bay Packer.

"Where you been?" I yelled.

He told me to get in and asked if I was free for the next couple of hours.

"Hell, yes!"

He drove out of Beachport to the Sunrise Highway for Manhattan. He didn't answer my questions and I could see that he wasn't feeling good.

"I tried to get to you last week, Franklin," I said.

He wasn't talking. He didn't even have the radio on for the race results.

"I was scared."

"What about?"

"You know what. . . . I had my final exams and everything."

I looked at him at the wheel. He had his tan gloves on. I was waiting for him to ask how I did with the exams.

"I thought maybe you'd been picked up."

"Flew down to Miami to see the lawyer. . . ."

I waited but he didn't say any more.

"I had these exams and I studied every night and weekends."

"How'd you do?"

"Okay."

"You going to pass?"

"Hell, I had all the answers."

"What's that mean?"

"I wasn't going to let that bullshit get me down. So me and Sam Schwartz, a fellow I know, we broke into Miss Robin's desk and got the test questions for history. And I worked up the damndest crib for English you ever saw. I had a phony fountain pen with stuff taped inside the top, and I had this poem 'Hail to Thee Blithe Spirit' on black paper fixed to my sock." I grinned and stretched my arms out like a prizefighter who'd just won by a knockout. "It was a pushover."

I waited for some good-boy stuff but he clammed up.

What had I done? What had pissed him off? I couldn't think of a thing, except maybe Vincy. But she wouldn't dare tell him.

"I did it because you said you needed me to go to college."

He was driving like the other time, in and out of traffic lanes, pushing through changing lights. His hands, which usually just touched the wheel, held it like he was choking someone.

"How's your kid?" I asked.

He gave me a quick look and I had the feeling that I was out of line, so I dropped that and tried talking about the Dodgers and Jackie Robinson and Marion Motley, the big fullback for the Cleveland Browns. Did he think that meant more colored players in the game? He was still buttoned up.

I always liked the 59th Street Bridge, so I gave up trying to get him to talk and watched the steel struts flash by and the buildings on the river light up with the afternoon sun. I promised myself I was going to live in one of those snazzy joints someday. Not that I'd want to show off, but since I'd travel a lot it would be a great place for the folks whenever I came home to roost for a week or so. I'd have a hideaway for the chicks, maybe down in Greenwich Village or even up in Harlem on Sugar Hill.

I'd invite Eddie Norris and Sam Schwartz over for a poker game with Franklin, Hobie, and Hayes. Eddie would raise hell with me for spending all that bread when workers were starving. He'd probably be living in some crappy walkup, putting out leaflets and soapboxing in Union Square with big-lawyer speeches about justice. He was a good guy and all that and I was for the underdog; but the Negroes were the underdoggest of them all, and if I was going to do anything it'd be for them. I mean, if I really wanted to, with my silver bullet, I could be a real help.

"You think Joe Louis can beat Walcott?" I asked out of nowhere. My mind was going all around chasing itself because I was worried about Franklin not talking.

Franklin turned off Fifth Avenue at Rockefeller Center and parked in front of a row of private brownstones near Eighth Avenue.

"Let's go," he said, looking at his gold wristwatch.

"Where we going?"

"Just let's go."

He had the key to the front door of one of the houses and we climbed up two flights to another door. He opened it and I followed him into a large room that smelled of perfume and reefers. One wall was covered by a mirror that went from floor to ceiling. There were a couple of easy chairs, a table, and a double bed. Through a half-open door I saw the can, and in a corner near the bed was a tripod for a camera.

"What we going to do here?"

"Take it easy. You'll see."

It got to me like a mystery movie. I looked around, fiddled with the tripod, sat on the bed, and felt nervous.

Franklin slumped into one of the chairs and I caught myself in the mirror. Not much of a face, I admit, with a funny nose and ears that were large. (I was always bugged by the size of my ears.) I moved around to get a better look. Franklin watched me with something in his eyes, like they hurt. I was about to ask what we were waiting for when I heard a click. Suddenly through the mirror I saw Vincy and a man in another room; they were kissing and feeling each other up. I turned to get out of the room.

"Watch it," Franklin said sharply, grabbing me by the arms and turning me back to the mirror. "You can see them but they can't see you."

"I don't want to see them!"

"Why not? You wanted to see when you followed them."

The man was taking off his pants. Vincy was already down to her lace see-through panties.

I tried to break Franklin's hold.

"Cool it!" he said. "I'm not going to let you miss a trick. This is cold, cold turkey."

The man said something and Vincy laughed. I wanted to tear my ears off, to stick my head through the glass. I kicked and squirmed and begged to get out of there.

"Want your bullet?" Franklin said. "Want to be a winner? Your own boss? To know who you are? You want to be a real free man or you want to be in a chain gang like Emperor Jones? Get the greens out of your soul, boy! *Get it out!*"

"I'm going to throw up."

"Throw up!"

I tried to keep my eyes shut but I couldn't and I began to vomit my gut out. Vincy and the john twisted together on the bed like white snakes. That's the last thing I saw.

I was on the floor, gobs of stink on my face and hands. I was working my throat with nothing left to throw up. I tried to get to my feet. Franklin was cleaning me with a towel.

"Knock it off!" Franklin said.

He sat me down in one of the easy chairs. I pulled my legs up under me and closed my eyes. I wanted to disappear, but I kept bouncing around like a ball in a pin machine, this way and that way, and I couldn't stop bawling.

"Shut up," Franklin said and turned a switch. The mirror became blank.

After a thousand years the door to the place opened and Vincy came in alone. She didn't look at me but leaned against the wall, straightening her skirt.

"I want to go home," I said.

"There's no hurry," Franklin said.

What could I do? He was boss. He was the Word.

"What about Vincy now?"

I looked hard at her. She was more beautiful than I had ever seen her. She wore a silver jacket over a light blue skirt. A silver band across her hair. Jee-sus! But I wasn't going to show her how I was feeling.

"She ought to get back to Em's," I said, pushing my voice as hard as I could. "You don't want her to lose any trick time, do you?"

Franklin smiled like he had won a 600-to-1 combination. "Doc's right, sugar."

She didn't like that, but she got up and fixed the scarf around her head. "You give me a lift, Franklin?"

"What's the matter? Didn't the john leave you any yellow money?"

"I want to ride with you."

"Not going your way. Doc and I've got business."

"What's the matter, Franklin, man?"

"I'll take it up with you later."

"What I do?"

"I told you to lay off Doc, didn't I?"

I had to put him straight. "I kept after her," I said.

"She takes orders from me. I warned her."

"But it's my fault," I said.

"What the hell, you had hot pants. That's no fault."

"I'll keep away," I said. "I don't even want to see her again." The words came out of my mouth. I could hear them. But cold turkey or not, Vincy was still there in the head.

"Come on, boy. I want you to meet Brian."

"Who?"

"My son. I brought him up from Miami. Going to stay with me a while."

Suddenly I felt blood in my head. What was he doing to me? Break me up with my girl? Bring another kid in to take my place? The greens I had felt for Vincy grabbed me like a 105 fever. The next thing I knew I jumped for him, batting my head against his belly, flinging my fists into his chest.

He took it without fighting back. I tried to see if he was hurting. He looked down at me as if I was a fly buzzing around. When I couldn't raise my arms anymore, I tried to kick him. He pushed me away. I came back at him. Again he pushed me away, saying, "Cool it, Doc!" I didn't stop. And the next time I moved in, he pushed me against the wall so hard I fell to the floor.

"Okay, man," Franklin said, kneeling next to me. "That's it. You've had your run for the day."

He took my arm to help me up but I pulled it back and got to my feet. I was still angry. Vincy, standing in the corner, said, "Lay off him, Franklin! He's only a kid."

That hurt but I didn't want to think about it. "How long is Brian going to stay?"

I was suddenly tired and a little scared. I sat down on the

edge of the bed, facing away from the mirror. One thing I didn't want to see was myself.

"Listen, Doc, and listen with two ears and your brain. What I'm going to say to you is gospel but without the music. I know what got your pecker up. Sore at Vincy. Sore at me. Nobody likes teachers that hurt. But you got to learn that a little pain never really hurt nobody."

"You have Brian up here with you. You don't need me."

"Shut up and listen. You got too close to Vincy and I warned you about that. But you let your balls run you. And you've come to the end of that line. You're not so smart, Doc. You'd end up a pimp. Once you let it all out to a whore or any dame, you're her pimp for good. No matter who you are. Rich man, poor man. . . . When you're pussy-whipped you don't even believe what you believe."

In any serious fight, words or fists, he once said, never stop attacking.

"Bullshit," I said.

"You got the greens about Brian too," he went on, not hearing me. "You think he's going to move into your spot. And you've grown to think you got a call on Franklin Gilboa. Want me all to your living self! Not Mr. Gilboa, boy. I told you that before but you weren't hearing me. . . . I could see it coming when I first talked about my son. You didn't like it. But as long as he was in trouble a thousand miles away, okay. But now he's here. Living with Papa. Zambang! Old Doc hates that. Hates it worse than seeing his girl screw a john. Tries to bat down old pal Franklin. I saw killing in your eyes. If you had a gun or a shiv, you'd have tried, wouldn't you?"

"No. . . ."

"Eyes don't lie."

"I swear—"

" 'I swear I didn't mean it, judge,' " he said, mocking me. "You're not funny, kid, but you're making me laugh."

130

What was there left? Everything he said was true, except I wouldn't have killed him even if I'd had a gun. Not Franklin. No more than I'd hurt Pop.

"You're not with me. Listen!"

"I'm listening. . . ."

"I'm one teacher got to learn from himself. And what I learned is this—people who get too stuck on each other generate a helluva lot of heat. Heat changes the shapes of things. That makes me real uncomfortable. I don't like it any way from seven. I go for cool. Space between people. A little air. Open up the territory."

From the window came fire engine sirens. He pointed with his broken thumb to the sound as if they were making his argument for him.

"Doc, I liked you—and I like you now, even if you are a crazy kid. Even had plans for you, as I've told you. But things, as I say, got too feverish for my taste. Bothering to break you from Vincy. Then Brian. No, sirree. When I felt you butting your head against me, boy, I knew we'd come apart."

His eyes were half closed and he looked sad. I was ready to throw myself at him, to beg him to stop talking. He couldn't be meaning it.

"Doc—" He had his hand out. "I'm not liking this either. . . ."

"You said you needed me."

"Not that much."

"But I was helping you. I was your silver bullet."

"A story, kid. Let's shake and get it over with. This is getting-off time."

I wouldn't shake his hand. I thought: He's conning me. That's what it was. Seeing how I'd take it. I gave him the old smile. But he turned away to Vincy and told her he'd changed his mind. He'd take her to Em's. I began to feel real cold and my teeth and hands shook.

"Franklin. . . ."

"If you ever get in trouble, kid, honest-to-God trouble, Em'll always know where to reach me."

"No!"

I wanted to cry but I wouldn't, sure he was testing me. To see how cool I could be. "Okay," I said. "I guess I'll drop out of school."

He laughed. "You're conning the wrong fellow. If you want to cut your own throat, I'm not handing you a knife but I'm not stopping you either. Let's go, sugar."

Vincy had tears in her eyes but she nodded and said to me, "Take it easy, lover."

"Be sure you close the front door tight when you leave," Franklin said, and he walked past me, big as a mountain, his shoulders swinging, his eyes with not even a blink in my direction. Everything I loved walked out of the door.

I waited, hearing the sound of their steps down the stairs. I was sure they'd come back. I waited. The front door slammed.

"Sonuvabitch!" I cried.

Then it all fell into place. I'd be what he wanted me to be. Cool. Real cool. That was the game. It was all a game. Me, Franklin, Vincy, Em, the johns, school, Pop, Mom, Marcy. . . . It was like Houdini, like the magicians at Loew's Beachport on Saturday matinees. It was a setup, a trick. That's what they called the johns, tricks! The trick is that the closer you watch, the less you see. If you let yourself go, start believing, get inside, you get fooled. You got to let the "magic" go by, stand off, don't lay into it, don't even try to understand how it works, and then you can laugh when the fellow puts everything back into his black bag and hands it to the pretty girl with satin tights and big boobs. You place your bets and you're going to lose sooner or later, so don't put your whole bankroll on any horse or any number or anyone with two legs. Don't fall in love! Take it all! Eat it all! Just roll it around in your mouth without swallowing. Keep your fingers warm, your pockets loaded, your ass tight, your eye on the second hand. It's now, this minute, baby. Fuck tomorrow. Fuck love. Fuck Franklin! I was cold-turkeyed and cold-cocked. I was on my own, I was free!

Then, not even knowing I was crying out loud, I picked up an ashtray and threw it into the mirror. It broke into a million pieces and me with it. Who the hell wanted to be free?

16 The question was: How long can a fellow keep cool and hating at the same time when the inside is burning and the outside isn't frosting fast enough? God knows, I tried to remember how I felt, bringing up in my mind Vincy and Franklin and what he said when he ditched me and walked through the door. But I found that being cool doesn't last, at least not with me. I had lost it when I broke that mirror, hating Franklin. But after a couple of days of moping around, things got awfully messy in my head. I was like a zombie or something, not wanting to eat or talk or go to the beach or movies. The truth is I was missing Franklin; my gut felt like someone kicked it whenever I heard jazz on the radio from Small's or the Cotton Club. At first I'd turn it off. But without my wanting to, the old fingers would crawl back to the knob. Weeks went by, me not knowing what I was doing half the time. The folks noticed it, and Mom said I needed a tonic or vitamins. Pop asked me to go to the track. I said no to both of them, although I was feeling lousy physically. Headaches, rotten pains in the legs, like a knife being jabbed into them. I took a lot of aspirin but it didn't help. Outside the house I had to limp, my legs hurt so much, but I kept all this from the folks, because the next thing I'd know old Dr. Rosenberg, the family doc, would come snooping by with his thick eyeglasses and black-and-white beard. I never could fool Doc R. and I didn't want to get sent to bed or anything. I had to be free to move around, because I hadn't given up on Franklin. I was going to find him and make up if it was the last thing I ever did. As a matter of fact, I went into Harlem one afternoon to the old spots but no one knew where he was. I stopped at Em's but she told me to forget it—and not to come around anymore. She said Vincy wasn't living there and wouldn't give me her new address. That was bad news too! I knew I had to look full time, not just a dab now and then.

The legs were killing me. The pain got worse at night and that pillow of mine sure caught some teeth marks. Once when there was a wind storm I went down to the ocean and screamed. It didn't help much, but it was better than not yelling. And I didn't really know if I was yelling because of my legs or Franklin or Vincy, or all three.

17 "What are you going to do this summer?" Eddie asked. We were sitting on burned-off pier stumps on the Sound, watching some jerky guys and dames on a Chris Craft trying to show off to each other. It was moored nearby, and they were mushing all over the place even though it was still light.

"I don't know," I said, wishing he'd learn to ask questions I could answer.

"Why don't you know?"

"I don't know, that's all."

"You got to begin to think about it."

"Shut up, will ya, Eddie!"

There was a girl on the boat who looked a helluva lot like Vincy, and I thought if I could see her now I'd be the happiest dude in the world.

I didn't know what to do with myself. I had to find some way of getting free to find Franklin, but I still didn't know how to work it. Without him, I was living in a black hole.

"What you doing?" I asked. One crappy question always leads to another.

"I'm going to Camp Red Hawk, like I did last summer. Remember?"

"Yes," I said, but I didn't at all.

"It's great," he said. "A lot of great counselors. Smitty, who plays guard on CCNY's basketball team, is coming back. And Hunch Meyers, who pitches for Penn. He's going to try out with the Dodgers when he graduates."

I guess he saw he wasn't winning so he threw in his reserves. "And a colored fellow who's a friend of Jackie Robinson's. He's going to coach swimming."

That didn't do it either.

"And listen, Doc, you know everybody's talking about how there's going to be revolution with the Reds all over the place. Not Socialists like my folks but Bolshies. Or a depression. And camp's a great place to learn how to live in the woods."

I never knew where he picked up his dope on things. Maybe there was stuff around like that in the papers, but I only read the sports pages and the only Reds I kept track of were in Cincinnati. And they needed some more hitters if they were going to make the race.

"Why don't you ask your folks to send you? The two of

us'll have a terrific time. And there'll be dames from a camp right across the lake. We have dances on Saturday night. We'll be seniors. . . ."

I could just imagine. High school girls with pimples and tight bras who'd be scared to death of going even halfway. They'd put me to sleep. And who cared about dancing with all the counselors around making wisecracks and fixing up dates for themselves with the counselors from across the lake? I'd had camp, believe me. When I was twelve. Camp Iroquois. Never again!

Eddie gave up after a while, and we lay back against the pier stumps and watched those assy types on the Chris Craft drinking beer and laughing at some stupid joke. Then Eddie said that if I didn't really get serious I wasn't going to graduate next year.

"Who cares?"

"You won't go to college."

"Great."

"Why don't you want to go to college?"

"Shit," I said. "It's just like high school except bigger. It isn't living, Eddie. It's books and a lot of talk, and a long way from where stuff's happening."

"What do you want to be then?"

Another one of those awful questions. Once I wanted to be like Franklin. Lots of dough, chicks, and no one to boss you. I still wanted to be like him.

"Yeah, so what do you want to be?"

"On my own," I said.

"Hell, that's no profession. I'm going to be a lawyer, you know that. To help people. To fight for the poor."

I thought about what Franklin told me once: "Poor folk is another country. There'll always be slobs who'll have less than other people. Give everybody a million bucks and in six months there will be some with five million. It's natural. Like the seasons. I don't mind helping the bastards, but I ain't going to fool myself into thinking that no matter how good things get there won't be those slobs living in that other country. That's humanology."

"If you work for the poor, how are you going to make a living?" I said.

Eddie thought about that for a while. "I don't know." He drew a six-pointed star in the dirt with his shoe. "I don't know. Sometimes I get all mixed up."

I gave myself a good laugh. If he was mixed up, I was going down the sink. "What do you say we play some pool?" I said.

"Let's go over to Jack's boatyard," Eddie said. "Maybe he'll take us for a sail."

The Chris Craft was out into the Sound, zigzagging toward Connecticut. I could hear the girls laughing across the water and I was feeling sad again.

"Still seeing that girl you told me about?" Eddie asked.

I wanted to tell him the whole truth, but he wouldn't understand. Besides, he'd think I was making it all up. I mean, how can you tell someone about Vincy and the mirror and me throwing up and passing out?

Later, on the way to Prosser Street, we stopped off to watch a parade. There were a bunch of Jews—rabbis, young kids carrying blue-and-white flags with the Star of David on them, and a couple of hundred others. They carried signs saying SUPPORT ISRAEL. FIGHT FOR THE NEW HOMELAND. BEN GURION WE'RE BEHIND YOU. A five-piece band from the Jewish Center was playing a song that no one could keep in step with.

"Jesus," Eddie said. "My folks are here. I said I'd march with them."

"What's the big deal?"

He looked at me like I was nuts. "Don't you know what's going on? The war with the Arabs."

"Sure. I hear the news. My folks are out of their skulls with it."

"Well?"

"Well, isn't it great?"

I saw an old couple walk by. It was the rabbi and his wife from a concentration camp who used to complain when I played handball against their wall. They were carrying flags too. An American flag and one from Israel.

"Sure, it's great," I said. "For the Jews in Europe."

"How about marching with them?"

"Hell, no."

"Why not?"

"How's it going to help beat the Arabs?"

He looked at me as if I was nuts.

When I got home, Eddie's pitch about camp kept noodling around my head. I figured that if I went to camp I could find a way of getting free—you know, con the director or someone and give myself time to find Franklin. Funny, isn't it? As soon as I settled on the idea, my headaches stopped, which was all to the good. But the legs still kept telling me they were there.

18 What Eddie Norris kept from me was that there would be flag raising every morning at seven and classes in Morse code, Indian history, and how to make campfires in the rain. There wasn't a goddamn thing taught there that would help in case the Reds took over.

But Camp Red Hawk was, as I saw it, a halfway station between Beachport and Harlem. I had told Eddie Norris when the idea hit me that I could be interested, so he sent his father to the house one night to talk it up. My father would do anything to educate his children, and I could see that he and Mom, worried as they were about my new quiet in the house—I didn't even fight with Marcy—thought that the camp would be good for me. I fought back but not too much because it's never a good idea to agree too quickly with parents on anything. Besides, in my case they would be suspicious. They kept selling me, and after a while I said if *they* wanted it I would give it a try. So my mother went out, bought a lot of camp clothes, spent a night or two sewing on nametapes, and I was ready for Red Hawk.

I didn't know then that my father had to borrow a couple of hundred bucks from my Uncle Jack to pay for the camp. But even if I had known, I don't think I would have changed my plans any. What I mean to say is that on the one hand I didn't want to hurt my father and put him to all that trouble—I felt kind of loyal to him too—but I knew in my gut that unless I found Franklin, and made up with him, I wasn't going to be good for anyone, Pop, Mom, or me. I'd have used my own money from the bank, but how could I without telling the folks how I got it?

Well, I suppose you know about these boys' camps. Hippity, hoppity, twitter, twitter, twitter—one big birdcage. Counselors making funnies which the kids laugh at to get on the right side of the big mucky-mucks, then soaping the kids up right before visiting day so they can get tips from the parents. March from tent to mess hall to swimming to tent to nap to baseball to flag lowering to campfire to tent, and if you don't do what you're told your group'll lose points and God help you.

At Red Hawk everybody griped at the food but food never

meant anything to me. The lake was passable but damn cold when we had to go for a swim after flag raising. The kids in my tent were zeros except for Eddie, and he lasted only one day because the counselor found out we were winter friends and he thought it better that we be separated, which didn't make me like him any more. He was a thin pimply guy from Rutgers with dirty brown hair. He thought he could make friends with us by telling us dirty jokes. I forgot his name as soon as I heard it. It was something like Seymour or Gerald—you know, one of those names like Melvin. I hated them all. I just called him "Hey." I don't think he liked me either.

Even though we were all seniors, the six of us in the tent, there was one guy from Boys' High in Brooklyn who pissed in bed every night. He couldn't help it and I heard some of the other kids call him stinko and pisher. What made it worse was that "Hey" thought he was being smart and could break him of bedwetting by making him carry his sheets out to the laundry, I mean, right through camp so everybody knew. I swear if I hadn't been planning to get out of camp soon I would have drowned the sonuvabitch.

In a week I had it worked out. There was a black dishwasher named Hippo. I told him that my grandmother on my father's side was a colored woman from Alabama, which explained why my hair was so thick, curly, and black. He got a day off once a week and hightailed it down to New York to check on his girlfriend. By the second week I gave him a letter to mail from town.

There is no point telling you exactly what was in it, but the idea was that it was supposed to be from my father to "Admiral" Abe Greenberg, the camp director, saying that there was a death in the family and that he thought Melvin ought to come home for a couple of weeks. And if Melvin did not return, then the "Admiral" could keep the balance of the tuition.

I was sure that the money business would make it sound real. A couple of days later right after flag raising "Admiral" Abe called me into his office. He sure was Navy; he was a sailor in the war. On the wall were pictures of Nimitz, Halsey, and the battleship *New York*. The "Admiral" himself was short and kind of fat, with a long nose that twitched a little bit at the end. I think the thing I didn't like about him most was that his hair was always slicked down and smelled of perfume or something, and he talked like he was ordering a whole fleet of flattops to surround the enemy.

"You can sit down, mate," he said. "Everything been shipshape with you up to now?"

"Fine. . . ."

"You like our craft?"

"Fine. . . ."

"Made some first-class shipmates? Great fellows all."

"Fine. . . ." (I always used that word when people asked me about school or how I was feeling. There's nothing better.)

"Well, sir, got a letter from your father this morning."

I tried to look real surprised.

"Your Aunt Rose—" He stopped for a moment and twirled a little ship's steering wheel on his desk. "You know, son, we always have to face tragedies in this life. It's like war. You lose a buddy, you lose a ship, you feel like Hades. But you got to keep on fighting. Life, war, they are like twins. Never surrender."

"Yes, sir. . . ." I wished he would get wherever he was going fast, because I didn't know how long I could keep that straight look on my face.

"Well, I got a letter from your father, and there's sad news. He's all right, mind you, and so are your mother and sister, but I am sorry to tell you, mate, that your Aunt Rose passed on to the beyond."

I didn't know whether to squeeze out a tear or not, but I

thought maybe I'd better try to look like I had some lake water up my nose. I could see he was watching me closely. I began to think maybe I had jumped the gun and I made a face and said, "You mean, she's dead?"

He nodded. He blew his nose and wiped his eyes, but I knew he was putting it on for my sake. "Your father thinks it advisable that you go home for a while—maybe two weeks. I am not sure it's the right thing for you, but after all father knows best." He stood up and walked over to me like he was parading and put his hand around my shoulders. "It's a tough break, mate, but as I said that is how things come. We'll miss you here at Camp Red Hawk, and I'm sure you'll miss us."

He began to sound a little bit like Al Jolson singing "Mammy." "And we'll welcome you back with open arms. Once a shipmate, always a shipmate."

"Yes, sir."

"I told your counselor to help you pack your trunk."

This I hadn't figured on. I sure wasn't going to lug the trunk all over Harlem, so I said quickly, "No, sir, I'll be coming back like you said. Better leave the trunk here, and maybe I can just borrow a knapsack."

He smiled. "You mean a seabag, don't you, boy?"

So I said good-bye to Eddie Norris, telling him about my poor Aunt Rose, and I drew out the twenty bucks that Pop put into the camp's candy and ice cream fund, added it to the seventy-seven I had, took the bus down to Pawling, a train to Grand Central Station, the shuttle across to the Eighth Avenue line, and hopped an A train for Harlem.

I always got a kick riding the A train. This time it wasn't too crowded. It was early for the maids and cooks who worked downtown. But there were other times during the day when riding up to Harlem was like diving into a hot pool. There was always some colored guy sleeping it off against the end wall, some young kids shooting the breeze so loud you could hear them over the wheels, and good-looking chicks wearing their go-to-movie clothes, spanking new against their dark arms and faces. I'd get a real kick out of seeing the big mamas, with their solid round black arms laying easy on their bellies or laps, moving their lips to read the ads over my head or working the inside page of the *News*. They might look worried or tired but never scared. I mean, you'd think they could handle anything that came their way, white or black, just by stiffening up a little and throwing a look as hard as a Joe Louis punch. But they were soft too. They had these big boobs and you'd feel if you were ever busted up over something and sad you could lay your head on them and get it all wiped away.

What was fun too was seeing how the color changed. At 42nd Street, it was mostly white. By 96th, white with a sprinkling of chocolate from the maids, cooks, and cleaning women from the rich people around Central Park West. By 110th, black, except for a few Irish. Above that, the car got blacker and blacker with maybe some Spanish or Puerto Ricans. Late at night when most of the passengers were sleepy, I imagined I heard above the noise of the wheels a different sound, like crowds humming and singing to themselves.

That day, sitting in the car with my seabag jiggling on the floor between my legs, I thought nothing could be strange to the colored people around me. They didn't look at me twice.

It was a damn good feeling to be on my own. I didn't know where I was going to sleep if I didn't find Franklin the first day, but there were a lot of places where I was known as Franklin's friend, and I was sure I could always end up at Em's even though I might be off her guest list. I had bought a pack of Lucky Strikes at the station and I stuck one in my mouth. I wasn't going to light it on the subway, but it felt good to just run it around the old lips the way Franklin did.

125th. 135th. I took a long deep breath and kind of danced off the train. Harlem, here I come!

19 It wasn't the easiest thing in the world to walk with my legs hurting and a seabag over the shoulders, getting heavier by the block. Harlem streets are hotter in July than anywhere. And wherever it's hotter, you can have it. The heat comes down out of every open window you pass, off the roofs, up from the subway gratings, all of it like a Turkish bath Pop took me to once, except you could walk out of the Turk's any time you wanted to. But not Harlem.

There was a breeze along the cross streets, drifting in from the Hudson to the East River, but the air was so hot it didn't make any difference. The heat shoved your breath right back down your throat. It was so solid you could cup it in your hands and throw it. (Hell, even my sweat had sweat.)

Franklin once told me that Harlem suffered more from heat and cold than anywhere, but that wasn't because it was black; it was because it was poor.

Everything was part of the heat—the kids yelling under the water from the corner hydrants, the radios bombing away from all the windowsills, fire engines, police car sirens. Even the smell of frying stuff. What I mean is that after a while I got this crazy idea that if the heat stopped so would the noise and smell. Or if they cut out, it would get cooler.

I dropped down to 134th Street and over to Seventh to The Bar to talk to John Hemingway. Franklin used to drop in there sometimes in the afternoon for a beer and some sweet talk with the chicks. I think he'd met Vincy there. Once in a while he'd connect with a good-looking chick on her own and work her up to doing herself a favor by taking him to her pad. If she was right, he'd live with her a while, then move her to Em's as part of his stable.

"Hey, Junior, how ya doin'?" John said when he saw me. He didn't ask me why I hadn't been around for a while. But that's the way it was. Nobody asked too many questions in Harlem.

The bar was half filled, mostly with dudes and their chicks waiting for telephone calls. In the back the pool tables were clicking away like a New York Central train.

John gave me a beer and I asked him if Franklin had been around. He gave me a kind of look I didn't like much. I knew it was a mistake. So I said I'd been away and out of touch, which was true. You had to level with John.

He made a couple of whisky sours for some customers, then came back to me. "Ya try Em's?" he said. "If she don't know where the Man is, I sure don't."

I went to the phone to call her but she sent word that she didn't know where Franklin was and didn't want to talk to me.

By eight o'clock that night I'd tried Hobie's and Hayes'— they were out—the Spot, the lobby of the Hotel Theresa, Eppie's Diner, the Chicken Shack, the Bar-B-Que next to the Apollo, Solly's Barbershop, the cashier at the Cotton Club, and the doorman at Small's. The people I knew and asked didn't know where he was and looked at me like I was a twin for J. Edgar Hoover. I was in trouble.

My legs were giving me holy hell and I was swimming in my sweat, so after a couple of hot dogs at Mary Sunshine's on Lenox and 117th I looked for a place to stay.

A lot of FOR RENT signs were stuck on ground-floor win-

145

dows, and I tried a brownstone on 117th Street between Lenox and Seventh. The stoop was crowded with kids shooting craps or playing tic-tac-toe for pennies. The hallway was dark and smelly. Stuck on a ground-floor door was a piece of paper saying MANAGER. I knocked two, three times and a fat old man, smoking a cigar, opened up.

"Yeah?"

"You got a room for rent?"

He pointed the cigar at me as if I was a walking ashtray. "What you want a room for?"

That was real nutsy, I thought, but I let it go. "To live in."

He didn't seem to understand, so I said, "I want to rent a room for a couple of weeks."

"How old are you, bub?"

"Seventeen."

"What you do, run away from home?"

"No, sir."

He looked down at the seabag in my hand. "Cops after you?"

"No, sir."

"Who is it, Webb?" a woman's voice said from behind him.

"Someone to rent."

The woman came to the door. She was a short dame with gold teeth, and a pot in her hands. She gave me a look like I was something the garbage man forgot.

"No kids," she said.

"I'm seventeen."

"I'm Eleanor Roosevelt," she said.

"That's the truth. I swear to God."

"He's big enough," the man said.

"Where?" she said.

"What you doin' up here?" the man said.

"I like it up here," I said, and I knew I'd made a mistake.

146

"Hah!" the woman said. "Ya on to somethin' else, boy. Besides, we don't rent to whites." She went back into the room.

That got me woozy for a minute and I didn't say anything. The man blew the cigar smoke into my face, though I don't think he meant anything by it.

"I'm looking for a friend of mine," I said.

"Who's that?" the man asked.

"Mr. Franklin Gilboa."

He yelled into the room. "Ya know any Frank Gilboa?"

"No!" the woman yelled back. "And close the door. Ya lettin' in all the hot from the street."

"Sorry, bub," the man said. He shrugged and giggled a little, which didn't fit his fat face. "She's the manager. I'm boardin'."

I limped down the steps and took a minute to lean against the stone banister. I was real bushed. The legs were giving me bad twinges and I was dry in the mouth and wet all over. I walked up the block looking for another sign. Now and then some hooker would give me a look and then maybe think twice and pass by. I guess I wasn't john stuff with my tennis shoes, khaki shorts, and shirt.

Around eleven o'clock I found an old lady in a walkup brownstone on 120th Street who was almost as white as I was. She said she'd rent me a room if I paid her two weeks in advance, which was ten bucks. The room was up four flights, small and dark, with a bed, a chair, and a washbasin. The toilet was in the hall. An alley filled with garbage and families of loudmouthed cats was just below me. Radios blasted from every open window; men and women were talking, laughing, screaming at each other, and yelling at kids. I hadn't had much to eat that day but my legs hurt too much to walk down the four flights. Besides, the smells of food coming up the alley made me a little sick to my stomach. I thought maybe I was a damn fool to be where I was instead of in my tent or with the guys swimming and roasting potatoes around the evening campfire. But I'd done it and I was going to find Franklin!

20 A day and a half went by. I limped and sweated all over Harlem, eating hot dogs and cokes whenever I was hungry. There was one place I hadn't tapped— the Regent Bowling Alley on 154th Street. Franklin owned a piece of it, and sometimes he would go there late at night to pick up cash.

I'm not wild about bowling. I don't know why, maybe it's just that you aren't really getting anywhere. You build up your score, but there's a limit. I mean, for Chrissake, you can hit 300 forever and be the world's champ, and that's that. In horseracing, on the other hand, there is always something you can't be sure of—the weather, the condition of the track, if the jockey had a fight with his chick or been snookered in a poker game the night before. All those things make racing open at the end and that's why I liked it. Besides, if you must know the truth, Franklin hated bowling too. He said, "If you put your finger in something round and black, it got to do more for you than make a lot of noise."

The place was crowded with bunches of kids having a tournament. What twerps! Each time they got a strike you would think they had won the Triple Crown.

Hayes saw me. He had his gold-rimmed specs on his forehead and he looked kind of worried.

"How ya doin', Doc?"

"Okay, I think."

"They tell me you been lookin' for Franklin."

"Yeah."

"He ain't been around. . . ."

"Is he sick or something?"

Hayes didn't know the answer, or if he did he wouldn't tell me. A couple of the twerps were hitting each other on the shoulders, yelling about how good they were.

"What d'ya want to see him for?" Hayes said.

I didn't know how to answer that right away so I took out a cigarette and tapped it on the back of my thumb like they do in the movies.

"I don't think Franklin's in the city, Doc."

That got me below the belt. Franklin leave New York? With his son? Wasn't I ever going to see him again?

"Where'd he go?"

Hayes looked at me like a teacher ashamed of some kid giving a stupid answer. "He didn't tell me."

A guy came over, took Hayes aside, and whispered something to him.

"Sorry, Doc, I've gotta get to work. If I see the Man, I'll tell him you've been around."

There was something going on, I was sure. Hayes used to be more friendly. Like he would ask me if I wanted a beer or, since it was so late, if I wanted to stay over at his place. I had this bad feeling. . . .

I started walking downtown toward 120th Street. It was a long walk for my legs. Half a dozen aspirin weren't helping me any. It was one of those hot, wet New York nights that can kill you. It had to rain sooner or later, and I wanted to get inside before it hit. So I limped along Seventh and when I got to about 140th Street I ran into a line of hookers. The truth is I was so wiped out that I couldn't have made it with Lana Turner or Rita Hayworth, so I kept ducking away until I heard a voice I knew.

"How about it, man?"

Vincy was coming into the street light. God, she looked awful. Her hair was in a bandana and she had this awful thick makeup on her face.

"Vincy!"

She began to laugh. Then she moved off. I grabbed her arm and pulled her to me.

"For Chrissake, Vincy."

She pulled her arm away. "Let me go."

"No. Gee, Vincy, I missed you."

"Look, buster. . . ."

"Don't buster me. I'm Doc."

A couple of hookers moved in. "Givin' you any trouble?" one of them said. She had a shiv in her hand.

Vincy looked at me and then at the hookers.

"It's okay." She began to laugh again and stopped suddenly. "You got a butt, Doc?"

I gave her my pack and said, "Let's go and have some coffee somewhere."

She lit up and stuck the rest in her pocketbook. "Don't have the time, boy. Way behind for the night."

"I got some bread."

"How much?"

"Enough."

She smiled and said okay. We walked around the corner to Danny's, a pimp hangout that Franklin had told me about. It was one of those places he called doghouses. It wasn't his kind of trade and he showed one to me to teach me the difference.

The place was hot and smelly. Vincy didn't want to eat; all she wanted was black coffee. In the light of the joint I could see her beneath the makeup. She was still beautiful. Hell, you don't change so much in a couple of months.

"What the hell gives, Vincy?"

150

She didn't answer for a while.

"I asked you a question."

"You seen Franklin?" she said.

"No, I'm looking for him."

"I mean, have you seen him since that day?"

"Nope. Know where he is?"

She knocked down the coffee and asked for a refill. "You gotta go home tonight, honey?"

"No. I'm living up here now."

She didn't seem surprised. "Want to go back to my place?"

"Sure."

"Let's stop off at Sammy's and buy us a bottle," she said with a little touch of the old smile.

21 It was a one-room, which she told me she shared with another girl who was away for a couple of days. Not much of a place—a little larger than the one I had—with a double bed and her own can. If she had a pimp, he sure wasn't taking care of her, because the place looked terrible. Even the two chairs were kind of ratty. On the wall was a color picture of Satchmo and General Eisenhower talking together.

As soon as we got in she opened the bottle and poured a couple of stiff drinks. I waited for her to pull off her dress and get into bed. But she sat down on one of the chairs and slugged the stuff into her. I didn't remember that she drank so much, but I didn't say anything. I just kept staring, trying to figure her out.

"What you doin' these days, Doc?"

I shook my head. "Nothing. . . ."

I began to feel I was dreaming. How could I be sitting in the same room with Vincy and not have my arms around her, nuzzling her boobs, and working up to fall into bed with nothing able to stop us? I mean, how could I be just a couple of feet away from her without wanting to tear her dress off and pull her shoes and stockings off and wrap her legs around me? It was sure funny just sitting there, not touching her.

"You thinking about hoppin' into the sack?" she said.

I didn't say anything.

"How much bread you got?"

I took out all the money I had and counted it. Sixty-five bucks.

"You can have it all," I said and gave it to her.

She took thirty and put it under the pillow. "I'm bushed," she said.

"What's the matter, don't you like me anymore?"

She took a deep slug from the bottle. "Ya want your money back?"

I laughed, not a real laugh but enough to say I wasn't thinking about money. The whisky was getting to me and I began to feel a little horny.

"Got any coke?" she asked, getting out of her dress. That's all she had on, except her shoes. Red shiny ones.

"No."

"Reefers?"

"No."

"Where ya been?"

"Home. . . . Going to school. . . ."

She jumped into the bed and lay back on the pillow. Her chocolate-milk body was right there. I took another mouthful of the stuff, sat down on the bed next to her, and put my hand on her flat belly. She moved away.

"Take my shoes off," she said, and watched me when I did it. I kissed the bottoms of her feet. She used to like that, but she pulled them back. "Why do you want Franklin?"

"Just to see him. . . ."

"I hate his guts!"

I was kind of walloped by how angry she was. "What gives?"

"Ya know what he did to me after the show we put on for you? Threw me out of Em's. Cut me down like I was a dog. From that time on I had to hustle the streets. No one'd take me in. The word went on the wire, Vincy's rotten. That fucker's gotta have everythin' his own way, just like he wants it. Hitler! He tells ya what to do. If you don't do it, you're on your ass."

She began to cry, the tears messing the makeup, and I couldn't take it. I put my arms around her and tried to kiss her but she shoved me away.

"He couldn't love another human being if he worked at it twenty-four hours a day. It scares him. I loved him. You did too. . . . Anybody love him, he runs. . . ." She groaned. "He's so hot, everybody around him gets hot. Then when ya get real close, he burns and we burn. He don't like that worth a shit."

I had my thoughts on other things. I wanted to get on, to make up for the lost time. I had a lot of backup in me.

"You'll be okay, Vincy. . . ."

"I'm workin' for five bucks. Christ, I used to tip bellhops five bucks."

I put my hand on her breast. She let it stay and didn't say anything. "I love you," I said.

She reached over, rubbed her fingers against my cheek. Tears kept dripping down her face and I wiped them away. "I haven't been laid since that last time," I said. I bent down to kiss her mouth and this time she pushed me back hard.

"On your way, buster!"

"I told you, I'm not buster!"

"Ya can have your lousy money back."

"I don't want it back."

"Beat it."

"I'm not going to beat it."

I swung over the bed and half covered her, her breasts in my hands and my mouth fighting to get to hers.

She bucked, twisting away. "Ya crazy bastard!" she said. "I'm sick. I got the red-white-and-blue blues."

"Oh. . . ." I let myself fall back alongside her.

"I'm not givin' it to you."

"Oh. . . ." I coughed hard like I was losing my breath.

"The dude who took me up gave me that little piece of poison."

I'd been sweating but suddenly I got cold. I mean, I really began to shiver. I put my hand up to my mouth to keep my teeth from clicking.

"You got to get fixed up," I said.

"Yeah, with what?"

"I heard there's a quick cure."

"Sure. But find someone who's got penicillin right now. And you need a helluva lot of bread for it even if ya get to the man."

"I'll find somebody," I said.

"You get me cured, honey boy, and you get all the free loving you'd ever want."

She drank some more and began to giggle and cough. I told her a lot of crazy things like not to worry, I'd take care of her. I wasn't shivering anymore, and I just kept looking at her, feeling sad. More than anything else I wanted her to get better so I could love her and be the way we were. Only of course this time it'd be different. I wouldn't be chasing her, jealous as a cat, driving myself out of my skull. No, this time it'd be different.

154

"Listen, Vincy, tomorrow you're going to stay in bed. I'll bring you some food and then I'll make connections with some doctor."

I could see she didn't believe a thing I said.

"You'll buy me another bottle too, won't ya, baby?"

"Yeah."

"You can stay here tonight, honey?"

"If you want me to, sure."

"I want you to."

She raised up a little bit, held her breasts in her hands. "You can come and kiss them," she said. "That won't hurt you."

Later she finished the bottle all by herself and began to cry again. I rocked her in my arms and tried to get her to cool it, but I didn't get anywhere.

22 I didn't do much sleeping. We lay naked without even sheets over us, it was so hot, and after a while we kind of just quit talking and she fell asleep. I heard her breathe and snore, sometimes groaning and moving her arms around like she was fighting off flies. I tried to figure out what to do next. In the morning I'd buy some groceries—eggs, canned salmon like we had at home, milk, bread, cokes. Make breakfast, boil water, put the eggs in them. I hate soft-boiled. If she wasn't up by then I'd leave her a letter telling her to stay in bed and when that was all done I'd go after Franklin. No matter how sore he was, he'd get her to a doctor who had penicillin. But where to start? Make the rounds again?

"Just so many bases a fellow has to touch," Franklin said

once. "No matter what he does or where he lives. You can tell what kind of dude he is by his tracks. Or vice versa." I wasn't sure I dug the "vice versa" bit, but I caught his meaning.

She was still sleeping when I came back with the food, and by ten-thirty, when I got out of the stinking subway and walked a couple of blocks to The Bar, it was hotter than the day before. Everybody was out in the streets even this early in the morning, thinking it would be cooler than later. Women were fanning themselves. Men, stripped to the waist, sweating, sat on stoops drinking cold beer or cokes; the kids had all the hydrants going and the mounted cops let them alone.

About half a block away I saw a crowd in front of The Bar. When I limped up I heard something I never thought I'd hear—Franklin pitching a small-time hustle. He was standing with his back to the window. On his head were some straw hats, one on top of the other, maybe half a dozen or more, and he was doing a spiel.

"Worth six or seven bucks in the stores on Fifth Avenue," he was saying. "Not a fire sale. Not a bankruptcy. Not a sale at all. But the right price for the right heads, brothers. One dollar!"

I worked my way behind a couple of tall dudes so he wouldn't see me. I didn't believe it. Not the Man. Not Mr. Gilboa!

"One pure dollar. And you'll be wearin' Rockefeller's hat. Or Frank Sinatra's." He handed one to a young dude and took his money. "There's a smart fellow. An' if you don't like Sinatra, old Satchmo wears these hats too."

It didn't take him more than a couple of minutes to sell them out. Then he said, "I've got eighteen bucks in my hand. Who'll match me, even money? Highest number on the first bill we take out. How about it, sports?"

No one spoke up.

"Make the odds better. My eighteen against your ten."

There was some shuffling around and whispering.

"Okay, man," said a fellow who was wearing a kind of sheet over his shoulders. He was a Jamaican.

"Let's get ourselves an honest judge," Franklin said, moving around and through the crowd. Then he saw me.

His face didn't show a thing. "Here's a young fellow from downtown. He may be white but that don't figure him crooked. Look at that face. How about it?" he asked the Jamaican, who gave me the onceover, said it was okay, and reached into his pocket.

"Hold it, friend," Franklin said. "The bill we take out first is what we're playing with. No dice looking at 'em."

The Jamaican took his time thinking it over, but the men around him yelled that it was fair, to get the money up. He took out a ten-dollar bill and gave it to me. Franklin's bill was in my hand already.

"Read it, kid," a man shouted.

"Loud and clear!" another yelled.

I read the Jamaican's bill. "Fourteen million three hundred thousand five hundred and five." Then I held up Franklin's. "Nineteen million—" I didn't get any more numbers out.

The Jamaican grabbed both bills out of my hand to read them. Franklin was right alongside him, ready to knock him about if he tried to run away. With a grunt and a curse the Jamaican turned the money over to Franklin.

"Don't go away, folks," Franklin said. "I've got twenty-eight of Uncle Sam's best products right here. I'll bet it all two to one on the smallest number. No looking first. Your fourteen against my twenty-eight."

I thought it was crazy. But some slob with a white vest on his bare chest insisted that someone else be the judge.

"Hey, John!" Franklin yelled into The Bar. "Come out here a minute."

John Hemingway came out, the silver patch over his eye shining in the sun. Franklin explained the deal and John said okay, he'd check the numbers if it was all right with the other party. Both bills were put in his hands and Franklin won again.

"Thank you one and all," he said, stuffing the new money in his pocket.

The Jamaican said, "I'll match you again on the last number. High man wins."

"Sorry, friend, but I got to get me to the track before they finish the morning workout." Then, before anyone could say anything, he ducked into The Bar behind John, who took his own sweet time at the door. I waited a minute, then ran in. Franklin was heading for the fire exit on the side. He saw me but didn't stop.

His white Caddie was parked in the alley. I jumped in.

He didn't say anything until he had cut onto St. Nicholas Avenue and headed downtown. He was exactly as I had seen him last, dressed good, with a bright red tie, a white seersucker jacket, and a straw hat with a red band. As he drove, he watched the people on the sidewalks as if he was looking for someone. But he was sweating hard. His skin looked greased and he wiped his cheeks and eyes with the back of his hand and swished the wet off into the air.

"What you want?" he said when we got into the park at 110th. He wasn't friendly.

It wasn't going to be easy, I knew, and I had to go slow, keeping Vincy until later.

"I wanted to see you again," I said.

"Why?"

"A lot of reasons. . . ."

"Start with number one."

158

"Jesus, Franklin, I hated when I didn't see you anymore. It was rotten. I didn't know what to do with myself. I thought I was going nuts. I even thought once I heard you yelling to me—in Beachport. It was all in my head. . . ."

He didn't say a word and watched traffic closer than I'd ever seen him.

We reached 72nd Street. He got out at Fifth Avenue and headed toward 59th Street. He turned the radio on for any news of scratches at Belmont.

"So you come mousing around Harlem, eh?"

"I wanted to find you."

"You told me that already."

It was going to be tougher than I thought. "We were friends," I said, hating the way I sounded.

"I told you, I didn't need a friend who wanted to eat me up. Was better we split. I told you that, didn't I?"

"Yeah. . . ."

"So what do you want?"

I never saw him like that before. His eyes were angry. What if he stopped the car and told me to scram? What would I do? He seemed to be steaming up from inside. There was only one thing left to say.

"You in trouble?" I said, trembling.

"What you talking about?"

I didn't say anything.

"Because you saw me do a little street pitch? Didn't I tell you there's always a down with the up? Bread one day and stones the next?"

"You told me."

"Did I tell you I was the greatest flatfoot hustler in town? You know what that is?"

"Uh-uh. . . ."

"It's working the streets until your feet get flat."

I was sure he was conning me.

"You get up in the morning with a sour mouth and your pockets filled with nothing but cigarette dust. That's all. Not a bent dime. Well, you're not going to let that stop you, are you? Specially when you got a sweet three-year-old running in the fourth at Belmont. You listening?"

Was I! But I couldn't believe what I was hearing.

"You need some bread, lots of it, maybe a grand right away. How you going to get it? Nothing's left for the three-ball man, and the word's out on the wire that you're dodging a bad nigger who's got himself a big hit. Not really dodging, understand, not Mr. Franklin Gilboa, but just leaving it lay a little. And you've picked up on all the cookie jars that're around from friends and neighbors, so you put on your sassiest duds, shave real sharp, slick a little grease on the hair, and look around for an oyster. In a little while you're having a free beer at The Bar and you happen to see out the window a kid about your age, Doc, heist himself a couple dozen straw hats off a delivery truck. The truck rolls off and the kid's heading for The Bar to do a little retail selling. I have to move fast, so I see a hooker who used to work for me and I hit her for a quick fiver, which is all she's got. I meet the kid right outside and offer him five for two dozen. He wants more, so I cut it down to eighteen and we've got a deal. That's when you came along."

It couldn't be, I thought. It had to be something else. Taking five bucks off a hooker and selling hats on the street? Not my Franklin.

He looked a little easier after he finished talking. Like the steam in him had sizzled out. When we reached Third Avenue he double-parked around the corner of a side street and said he was thirsty. We went into an orangeade and hot dog joint. I thought that he'd loosened up and soon I'd find the right time to talk about Vincy.

23 The usual Nedicks orangeade place was okay. That is, if the neighborhood was okay. You even got dabs of real orange in the juice. But this place was something out of a fire sale. I didn't see the sign but it couldn't have been Nedicks, which I knew from hanging around the ones in Beachport. The dog behind the counter, and I don't mean a frankfurter, looked like she just came back from a funeral. Besides, she was lumpy in the wrong places and squirted out the juice into glasses like it was spit. Franklin always liked good eating joints that were clean, so he must've been hit with a big thirst all of a sudden or he was going to meet someone there. He took out a scratch sheet, studied it, and after ordering another couple of orangeades and hot dogs he went to a booth to make a call, coming back in a few minutes looking real hustled. His eyes went over a few chumps at the counter and a horse-faced mick at the door lighting a cigar. With his chair back to the wall, he seemed to be looking for someone through the big dirty window. The street buzzed with lots of people sweating and hurrying, hurrying and sweating. Christ, I'd never really thought about how people seemed to be running all the time and who the hell knew where they were going. Not even them, I bet. I'd begun working on things like that after Franklin went away.

"You came at the right time," he said, sticking the scratch sheet into his pocket next to the *Racing Form*. "Hi-ho silver bullet. Riding to the rescue. Not that you can solve the problem, but I always figured you were a kind of good-luck piece."

He didn't sound real happy, but I felt better. Like the old times when he needed me. Or said he did.

"I'm going to tell you a story. You listen, hear? I'm telling it out loud so I can hear it too. Helps me."

He doused a gallon of mustard on his franks, which the slob brought over and dropped on the table.

"Couple of months ago, maybe six weeks, a real hot dude calling himself San Juan Joe came into the shop and put fifty bucks on a combination. Three eighty seven. I'm never too jazzed up with that big a piece. If it hits, it pays mighty big. So I laid off part of it with Hayes and Hobie and a couple of others, and with the chances 999 to 1 I didn't lose any sleep. Then the next day he came back with another fifty. I laid it off again. Day after day the same mouthy guy came back, always with some ass-licking friends, and threw the fifty on the tank for the same number. I tried to talk him into cutting down the bet, but he gave me some smart-ass jive about whether I was running policy or playing tic-tac-toe. I told him, 'I'll take your bread and eat it toasted.' "

Franklin looked up quickly when two colored guys came in. I could've sworn he was scared and it made me sick to think so. Besides, he was sweating again and couldn't get enough of the lukewarm juice to satisfy him. I had figured how much a fifty-dollar combination bet would pay off. It was 6 to 1 on the first number, 60 to 1 on the second, and 600 to 1 on the third. That added up to a helluva lot of dough—thirty grand!

"Now, you know how it works. Sometimes I'd look at my other bets to see how many threes were in, or how many thirty-eights or three eighty sevens. If I was light on them, or if there was no other three eighty seven, I wouldn't bother to even lay off the bet. I figured I had the odds. Well, so it went. He'd come in with his fifty, make some hot talk about how he'd get it all back soon, and I'd do the figuring and know I was safe. He'd laid about two grand and I was kind of taking it for granted. No sweat. One day—" He made a face and chewed a butt, pressing his lips together like he'd tasted garlic, which I hate. "One day just after he made his bet I got a call from a guy I knew at Jamaica. He said there was a push on a horse in the first race, Homing Pigeon. He told me to hurry out to take a looksee for myself. He couldn't say why on the phone but he wanted me to have a word or two with the jockey. It was going to be big—20 to 1."

I tried to jump ahead of the story. "A fix?"

He went on. "Boy, I got the hots! You hear of a sure thing and everything fades. It's Christmas in July. I slambanged to the track. I had the word or two where it was worth something. A bugboy was riding and he had no weight at all. Homing Pigeon had won a few races at county fairs and this was his first run at the big time. The other horses were dogs. Homing Pigeon could be a hot one in a cold race. I was satisfied. I had the good old tickle in the back of the neck and it was all I needed! So I bet the day's take from the shop—twenty seven hundred—which brought the odds down to 18 to 1, but who cared?"

The slob came over to get paid, saying the boss was coming by soon and if the cash wasn't in the register he'd raise hell. Franklin gave her the money with a fifty-cent tip, which sent her eyes rolling back. She almost kissed him, which would've been a lousy dessert. Franklin always was a big tipper. "Got to juice up the working class," he used to say. "Otherwise who'd have the cash to support the hustlers?"

"A couple of minutes before the horses got onto the track, I remembered I hadn't laid off San Juan Joe's bet. I ran back like a wild man under the stands to get on the phone to Hayes."

I knew what was coming. All the phones were locked up. No one makes a call unless you can prove an emergency, and even then someone's listening in to keep the race results from getting to bookies on the outside.

"Homing Pigeon sulked and hung there like he had put down roots," Franklin said. "It was my day in hell. Three eighty seven came in and I didn't have a dime laid off."

It was like hearing a curse, the way Franklin talked. I wanted to put my head down on the greasy table and die. His face was in the shadow of the wall so I could only see the eyes. Like they were fighting not to burn up. If I could reach over and touch him to tell him how I felt, it would be better than anything I could say. But I didn't move. I was afraid he'd pull away because I was getting too close.

"Shit!" I said. Which I admit was a nothing way to put what I was feeling.

Franklin leaned forward into the light. I'll be damned if he wasn't smiling. Not exactly a smile but kind of a half-assed grin.

"I'm sailed past the anger, boy," he said. "Blame it on no one but Mr. Gilboa Esquire. No gambler worth a sugar tit would turn down a horse with a push on. It took everything else out of my head. Not even pussy's in the same department. That's me. Wouldn't have missed that 20-to-1 shot for the president of these United States. If he'd called. But Mr. Gilboa has to pay off too. Thirty grand. Well, boy, Mr. Gilboa didn't have that in his pocket. All I had was a grand I suckered out of Hayes, one grand left from the day's take, two from Em, and one from a stash I had somewhere. Called my bankers, Venturi and Katz, but they were out of town over the Fourth. When San Juan Joe turned up next morning with his tail of leeches, I gave him the five grand and told him I'd pay him the rest the end of the week, three days away."

He rubbed his hands against each other, the broken thumbs sticking out.

"But Joe, he was hot. Mouthed it all over the place, sashaying around. Did a real floor show for the boys. Said he wanted the money right then and there. I could smell his perfume and blood across the room. But I had my .38 where it was handy. We nose-to-nosed for a while, with him yelling. Then he backed away, saying he was a good guy. He'd give me the three days, and if I didn't have it all then he'd take it out of me in the cemetery. . . . The three days are up today—and he's out there someplace waiting for me."

"What you going to do?"

"I got me an appointment eight o'clock tonight with my bankers."

"What we going to do until then?"

"Go to the track with this hat money and see how much we can make it grow."

I shook my head. He couldn't make it grow enough dollars' worth, that was a cinch.

"You know something," he said. "When Joe okayed the three-day deal I had this feeling there was a fix in it somewhere and I was Master It. I checked it with some of my friends around Small's, the Fat Man's Bar, Obie's. Nobody knew a thing."

"What about your friend who gave you the tip on Homing Pigeon?"

Franklin got cool all of a sudden. "I looked for him after the race, but he wasn't around. . . . Nowhere. . . ." He looked at his hands. "The whole thing was a fix—the race and the winning number."

He laughed suddenly like he'd thought of a good old joke. "Funny thing, Doc, your best friends are the little people. Guys and dames who play policy for pennies. Or the winos you bought a bottle for. Or the hookers you put into the trade when they were broke. The others—" He spit a piece of tobacco on the floor. "The others—" He let it drop like he had his hand on a burning match.

24

Franklin was a damned good handicapper, but when it came down to betting on a horse to win he let himself drift a little, like he was picking up messages from the way a horse moved in the paddock or on the way to the gate. His eyes would close and he'd rub the back of his neck slowly. He let three races go by without a bet. In the fourth race at a mile he watched a chocolate-brown filly named Doll Baby out of Kinder and Tarheel. She was 12 to 1 and had run fourth two weeks before at Jamaica and third to Assault at Pimlico. She was carrying a fair amount of weight but was lightfooted around the paddock and on the field. I loved seeing the shine on her neck. Eddie Arcaro was up, though he hadn't ridden her before. Franklin studied her under his half-closed eyelids; he was breathing heavy and sweating, chewing a cigarette into shreds. Just before they got to the gate, he counted out his money and gave me sixty bucks. "Run down, boy, and stick it on her nose. She's no morning glory."

At the window Doll Baby's odds had fallen to 9 to 1. Arcaro was doing it. He had taken elephant bites, as they say, in a lot of purses.

Franklin seemed asleep when they broke, but I was yelling and praying that stupid old prayer, "God, bring her home!" I rode that chocolate filly every step of the way. She got her first call at the turn. Fourth to Marie Hall, who was leading by two lengths. I screamed but I didn't know what I was screaming. At her next call she was second, neck to neck with Susie B., who was coming up fast while Marie Hall faded. I couldn't make her out at the far turn. It was like a dream when you think you see something but it's too dark to be sure. I wasn't even hearing the call anymore. Names were coming over like it was one horse. The yelling all around me made me deaf. Then suddenly I heard: "Hold your tickets." The stewards had posted an inquiry sign! I looked at Franklin, who had his eyes on me. He was smiling.

The waiting got to me. I thought I ought to get the ticket ready, just in case, but I couldn't find it in my pockets. God, if I lost it and she won I'd kill myself.

The announcer's voice: "Susie B. is disqualified for bumping during the stretch run. Doll Baby is declared the official winner."

I think I yelled but I'm not sure. I was still searching for the ticket when Franklin held it out to me. "Go on, boy, pick up the bread." I'd forgotten I'd given it to him.

He put five hundred away and bet the rest across the board on three more horses. We made another hundred on one place and one show.

"I knew you were my good luck," Franklin said as we fought our way through the crowd to his car. "Now let's keep it hot. If the rest of the day hangs together, tonight we'll twist the world back into shape."

Vincy was on my mind. I promised I'd get her fixed up and I had to start doing something about it.

"I saw Vincy," I said when we were out of the parking lot. "Last night."

"So what?"

"She's hustling the street."

"So am I. You get the highs and you get the lows."

"She's sick."

He didn't say anything, turned the radio on and off. I knew he was trying to decide something and I hoped it was on Vincy's side.

"She give it to you?"

"Hell, no. She just about let me kiss her."

"Got to go home tonight?"

"No. . . ." I was going to play this for all it was worth.

"Why not?"

" 'Cause I got me a room on 120th Street."

He slowed the car down and made a face like he'd swallowed a cherry pit. "What for?"

"So I'd have time to find you."

"Shee-it!"

"I'm supposed to be in some lousy boys' camp up in New York State."

"Who'd you con to break loose?"

I told him the story and I could see that he was kind of proud of me. He smiled a couple of times, especially when I told him how I claimed to be part colored.

"I want to get Vincy to a doctor with that stuff they give for syph."

"You still sugarin' for her?"

"Kind of."

"Hmmm. . . . That cold turkey didn't work?"

I didn't answer.

"You need a lot of bread for penicillin. You know now I don't have that kind of floating cash."

"Yeah. . . ." He was in a deep hole himself. "But could we stop in and see her? You know, make her feel good?" I was thinking about Dr. Rosenberg. Would he help? Could I trust him not to tell my folks? It was the only chance.

Franklin said he'd leave me off at Vincy's and come back when he was through with Venturi and Katz, his bankers. I asked why I couldn't go with him. How would it hurt? He laughed and said he didn't know how it would help. We argued back and forth and I knew I'd win because I'd learned that a gambler's always looking for a good-luck sign and I was Franklin's.

25 We got to 500 Fifth Avenue a few minutes before eight. Franklin signed the book in the lobby and we took the elevator to the fifteenth floor. We walked up the long hall to a door that said LAW OFFICES—CHARLES VENTURI AND SAMUEL KATZ. Underneath was a list of companies and corporations. Inside at a desk was an icy-looking white guy, dressed like it was winter outside—uptight tie, belted jacket, and creased pants so sharp you could cut steak with them. He said we were expected and Franklin told him he knew the way.

"That one in there's a bad boy," Franklin said after we walked through a small gate to a room in the back. He knocked. Someone yelled to come in. Two men were there. They gave Franklin a couple of phony hellos.

"Meet my friend Doc Henshel," he said.

Venturi was a pretty neat-looking guy for a fat man. Katz had pimples and was smoking a long cigar. Right away I didn't like him because he said, "Hello, Jew boy."

It never bothered me when one of the gang at Beachport called me that. You could always call him something back, like spic, wop, mick. But this was different. I hated it when a Jew did it.

"He's one of my best runners," Franklin said.

Venturi asked who wanted drinks. Franklin and Katz took scotch and I settled for a coke.

Through the open windows I could hear a fire engine and horns tooting.

"Where'd you fellows go over the Fourth?" Franklin asked. He'd put his straw hat on the floor next to his chair.

Katz said he'd flown to Chicago, which was no way to spend any holiday, and Venturi said he and the family went out to their place in Southampton.

"How's with you?" Katz said.

"Some dude got hot and hit big."

"Jesus," Katz said. I don't think Venturi liked his saying it. Italians are strict about religion.

"How much?" Venturi said, bringing over the drinks from a bar in a closet.

"A combination for fifty bucks."

"Whoa! Man!" Venturi said and gave me the coke.

"Thirty big ones," Katz said. He was leaning against a wall out of the light from the lamps but you could smell the cigar.

"I've paid off all but twenty-five. Some pickup bread and a couple of good days."

Venturi blew out his breath with a sizzling sound.

"I'll get it back to you soon at the usual ten percent interest a week," Franklin said.

"It's fifteen," Venturi said. "I told that to one of your partners."

"Okay, fifteen."

Katz clicked something against his glass and said nothing. Venturi sat down behind the desk and sipped the drink.

"Jesus," Katz said.

"I know how you feel, Franklin," Venturi said. "We've just had ourselves a real gut grabber. Something went sour in a land deal in Louisiana. Lost a big chunk. I'm really sorry for you. We know what it's like. How is it you didn't lay it off?"

"This fellow made his bet forty days running. I laid it off whenever the odds moved down. This one time I missed."

I saw that Franklin wasn't telling the whole story. That was okay with me, but Venturi and Katz, who sat down near the desk, looked at each other.

"That's not like you," Katz said. "You're a smart operator. I'm surprised. Really surprised. Aren't you, Charley?"

"I'm surprised," Venturi said.

"You weren't on top of things," Katz said. "Jesus, if you're not on top of things, who is? I'm surprised."

"Lay off him, Sam," Venturi said. "Everybody can make a mistake. Remember the case we had against Webster Construction when the judge asked us to bring those papers to court on Monday and we forgot and he gave us hell and found for the DA?"

"That *schmuck!*"

"And what about the time we paid a hundred grand for a piece of an air-conditioner company to find that the product could only make things hotter and never cool? Who isn't human, Sam?"

"I need it tonight," Franklin said.

"We haven't got that kind of cash in the office, have we, Charley?" Katz said.

"Not tonight."

"I'll pay off with one of your bearer notes," Franklin said. "The guy'll come by tomorrow to give it back for cash."

"It's a lot of money," Venturi said.

I think Franklin knew at that minute that he wasn't going to get banked. He got up from the chair and put his drink down on the edge of the desk. "You've done it before, Charley. More than twenty-five grand. What gives?"

"Nothing gives," Venturi said. Katz laughed and said that Venturi had made a joke without knowing it.

Venturi looked at Katz. "What joke?"

"Christ, Charley, I always told you you didn't have a sense of humor. There was a time, Franklin, when Charley here—"

171

Franklin said, "What's the score? You going to bank me or not?"

"It's not our money," Venturi said. "You know that. We have a fiduciary relationship with the lenders and I don't think we can make a decision just like that."

"You did it before."

"Not after a week when we dropped a quarter-million on that Louisiana land. We got to break that news first, and I don't see them dancing in the streets and running to pay out twenty-five grand for a mistake."

"They know I'm good for it. My credit—"

"Forget it, Franklin," Katz said. "They don't even know your name."

Franklin took a couple of deep breaths and wiped his mouth with a handkerchief. "You guys have made a lot of money off me."

"You've done pretty well yourself," Katz said. "How's Em doing for you? Our boys bankrolled that, didn't they? And how about the bowling alley? We bought in for you."

"And got paid back," Franklin said. He was steaming like before, and for a minute I was scared he might haul off and sock that Katz right out the window.

"I've got a crazy after me for the twenty-five. And it's coming to him. If he doesn't get it he'd like to cut my liver out if I let him. My name's always been good. I pay off on the dot. Every cent. Policy, horses, baseball, hockey—you name it. Franklin Gilboa's game was better than the mint. I had one hustle you could trust. Everybody in Harlem knows that. And you fellows tell me for a lousy twenty-five grand you got to call the big shots to okay it. Okay it, hell! I know where you get your bread from, you with your goddamn lawyers' diplomas all over the place. Where do the big shots stop and you begin?" He picked up his hat and turned to me, angry as hell. "What are we waiting for? Let's go."

"Hey, wait a minute," Venturi said. "Don't get on your high horse."

"Let's cut the bullshit. Going to bank me or not?"

"We can't right now," Venturi said. "Not the whole thing. Maybe a couple of grand. Okay?"

"Why don't you try the Guaranty Trust for the rest?" Katz said. I could've spit in his eye.

"But we know where you can get all of it. More even. That right, Sam?"

"On the nose. And every week."

"Some people who contacted us recently have a very interesting proposition to make for the right man up in Harlem," Venturi said. "They're looking for someone absolutely reliable, popular with the colored folks, but really honest, you understand, a straightshooter—"

"There he goes making jokes again," Katz said.

"Cut it out, Sam," Venturi said. "I don't see the humor."

"What's the deal?"

"A very good one," Venturi said.

"Are you boys in it?"

"No."

"What's the matter, not rich enough?"

"Very rich," Katz said. "But it's not our kind of law work."

Franklin straightened up like he knew what was coming. "Okay, what is it?"

Katz turned to me. "Go outside for a few minutes, Jew boy."

"Fuck you!" I said, forgetting where I was.

"Shut up, Doc!" Franklin said.

"Your little white friend's got a temper, hasn't he?" Katz said.

"Cut out the gutter talk, kid," Venturi said. "And do what Mr. Katz said."

Franklin said, "Anything I know he can know."

"Maybe we don't want him to know," Katz said. "Who the hell is he? We don't have business with him."

"I told you he's been running for me for years."

Katz threw his cigar in the wastepaper basket and lit another one.

"What's the deal?" Franklin said again.

"You understand," Venturi said after he finished his drink, "that we have nothing to do with it ourselves. We just want to put it your way because of our long association."

"Yeah. . . ."

"Well, these people are looking for someone like you. You'd be absolutely up their alley and I could guarantee if you went in with them you'd be making enough to set up your own bank, with all kinds of protection. You'd be kind of handling a big part of the operation in Harlem, a wholesaler, so to speak."

With the noise of horns and fire engines outside and Franklin speaking real quiet, I didn't hear what he said. But I caught Venturi moving his head up and down. Katz too.

"How about it, Franklin?" Katz asked. "We're doing you a favor."

Franklin ran his hands up and down the sides of his pants and I knew he was wiping the sweat off. "You know what you can do with your fucking deal?" he said. "I wouldn't handle drugs for a million bucks a day. I'd kill my mother first. Jesus, you boys are real sweet. Doing me a favor, huh? Stick it up your ass. I'm not going to touch drugs and everybody in Harlem knows it."

"Mr. Pure," Katz said.

"Easy does it," Venturi said, real cold all of a sudden.

"You're behind the times," Katz said.

"I'll tell you what, Franklin," Venturi said, going over to the closet to fill up his glass. This time he didn't ask what anybody wanted. "You're making a mistake. Bigger than not

174

laying off that bet. What we're talking about is going to be the biggest item in the country in five, six years. Everybody, I mean, everybody'll be wanting the product. Like Zippo lighters. It'll get so the kids in high school'll be getting the stuff at the corner ice cream store. It'll be the American dream, fellow, from top to bottom, whites and blacks, poor and rich, from Park Avenue to Hollywood Boulevard, from Seattle to Scatterbrain, Arkansas. We're giving you more than a favor. We're giving you your life."

"A rich man's life too," Katz said.

"As I said," Venturi said, "you've got the brains, the reputation for honesty and reliability. You've even got a lot of people up there believing in you. I know. Anybody you ask uptown—the cops, the preachers, the hookers, the working people—they say, 'We trust Franklin Gilboa.' Fellows like you don't come a dime a dozen. And we also know that some hardheads are eating into your policy territory. Sooner or later they'll take it all away from you. If it gets on the wire that you've reneged, you'll be way out in the cold. No matter who believes in you, you'll be pushing garbage for the Sanitation Department at thirty a week."

"If not worse," Katz said.

"Worse than drugs?" Franklin said. "You name it."

Katz started to say something but changed his mind.

Venturi went over to Franklin and touched his arm, trying to be friendly. Franklin moved away.

"What're you going to do if you can't raise the twenty-five grand?" Venturi said.

"I'll raise it."

"I wouldn't bet on that. . . . Listen to an old friend. You say this guy wants your liver. You wouldn't say so if you didn't believe it. Is it worth it? What'll you do, run away? Where'll you hide out? Philly? Chicago? New Orleans? LA? You know how fast bad news travels. America is one big

175

Harlem. Take our advice. See these contacts. Talk to them. Maybe you'll think it over."

"I'll tell you what I'm thinking," Franklin said. "I'm thinking that this is all shit. A setup. A fix. I think someone, maybe your contacts, banked that crazy with his fifty-buck bets for a straight forty days. Get me against the wall. And I think you nice clean white lawyers with your nice clean white hands telling me it ain't your kind of legal work are in it up to your clean white necks. So you tell your contacts to go shove it."

He turned, grabbed hold of my arm, and started for the door.

"Hey, boy," Katz called out. "Remember when they found out that a linotyper working at the *Daily News* was bribed by some policy gamblers to fix the last three numbers on the stock exchange reports? You know what happened to the linotyper?"

Franklin slammed the door behind him so hard I thought it would jump right off its hinges. When we passed the front desk, the guy with that buttoned-up suit was waiting. He called, "Hey, what's your hurry? I'm supposed to take you someplace."

"Up yours!" Franklin said. The elevator took too long to get there. Both of us were sweating real hard. I'd forgotten how much my legs hurt until then.

26 We didn't say a word when we got in the Caddie and drove up Fifth. The traffic was light and the night was as hot as the day. We passed a couple of horse carriages with people in them coming out of the park at 59th Street. I couldn't believe that anybody could be laughing and having a good time. Franklin looked scared and I wasn't feeling any good myself. Venturi and Katz had warned Franklin to play ball, that's what the story of the linotyper was all about. Somewhere out there San Juan Joe was looking for Franklin, and he had a lot of protection for whatever he was going to do.

"Don't let 'em worry you," I said, remembering the silver-bullet story.

"I've got to be out of sight until I think things over," he said.

"What about Em's?"

"That's the first place they'll look for me."

"You think Joe knows about Em's?"

"Any one of a dozen bartenders knows. They all take messages for me. It's not Joe anymore. It's bigger. You heard them in the office. They want my number. I know too much already. And so do you. I shouldn't have taken you with me." He reached over and touched my arm. "I'm sorry, Doc. You'll have to get out of Harlem. No later than tomorrow. Go home. Or back to that camp."

"No!"

"Don't fret me, boy. I got enough now!"

That shut me up but I wasn't going to leave. Not for a while yet. "What'll you do?"

He asked me about my room, who rented it to me and whether I'd seen anybody there I knew. Then he said he'd stay with me for the night and make plans. I felt great, even happy, not counting the trouble he was in.

"Could we stop off and see how Vincy is?"

He didn't like the idea, but when we got to her street he parked in a dark alley and said he'd go up with me for a couple of minutes.

177

The door was open. Vincy wasn't there. My letter was on the floor. I felt sad and gave it to Franklin to read.

"I can't figure it," I said. "Why didn't she wait for me?"

"Because she's a whore."

"What's that got to do with it?"

"They hate being alone. Got to be where the action is. Like gamblers. What can you do by yourself? Nothing. Besides, whores never know who they are. Nothing inside. They got to find something or someone to tell them. A john, another whore, a pimp." He saw the empty whisky bottles. "Booze is almost as good. But not enough."

I felt like crying. "But she's sick."

"Forget it, kid."

"I know where she's hustling."

"Let her go. You can't help her." He was at the door with his hand on the knob.

"I promised I'd get her a doctor."

"This ain't no time for the Red Cross, boy. You coming?"

We left. My place was only a couple of blocks away, and as we rode along Lenox I suddenly thought of his white Caddie. "Listen, Franklin. You don't want to park your car anywhere near my place. They'll stake it out."

He slowed down. "Christ," he said. "I'm not thinking clear." He made a U-turn and drove downtown to an all-night garage on 96th Street. He checked it in and we took a cab. No one saw us when we got to my place or walked upstairs to my room.

It was hot as hell. He stripped and lay down on the bed, hitting the flies coming in from the garbage in the alley. I stayed at the door. He looked at me. "What ya doin'?"

I was thinking of Vincy again. "Nothing."

"I'll sleep a bit and then give you a turn."

My mind kept going back and forth. Franklin—Vincy. Vincy—Franklin. I thought my head would split.

178

After a while I couldn't stand it anymore and said I was going to find Vincy.

He didn't say anything. He was a million miles away. I told him again and he looked up like he was seeing me for the first time. He seemed all burned out and I thought maybe I oughtn't to leave him.

"Lock the door and take the key," he said.

27 I found her on the same streetcorner but she didn't want to talk to me at first. I told her I had a doctor. She laughed and asked where the dough was coming from. Without thinking, I said, "I got this friend, Dr. Rosenberg. He'll do it for nothing." That stopped her and she said for me to call him. She'd be listening in to see if I was telling the truth.

It was past ten o'clock, but I had to take a chance. We went to a phone booth around the corner, and I made the call with Vincy sticking her ear next to the receiver. Rosenberg answered.

"Hello, Doc. This is Mel Henshel. . . ."

A big silence. Then, "Where are you?"

"I'm in New York. Just came in from camp."

"Are you sick?"

"No, sir. Just came in for a couple of days."

"Where are you?"

"I told you. I'm at a friend's house.

"Mel, you're lying to me."

"Okay, I'm in a phone booth."

"Mel, what's going on with you?"

"Nothing."

"Are you sure you're all right?"

"Sure I'm sure."

"Do you know you've driven your father and mother half crazy?"

That got me in the gut. Something went wrong. "What're they worried about?"

"You ran away from camp."

"I didn't run away."

"Mr. Greenberg called them to ask how you were and to give his condolences."

That nosy bastard!

"Look, Doc, I'm sorry the folks are worried."

"You go home right away."

Vincy looked at me with a Who-the-hell-you-kiddin' look.

"Doc, I can't go home right away."

"Something's wrong. Now, what is it?"

"Doc, I need your help. . . . I got a friend. . . . Well—Doc, you got this new medicine for VD?"

"Melvin, if you have it, you come right over."

"It's not me."

"You can tell me the truth."

"I'm telling you the truth. It's a friend. Have you got it?"

"Yes, but I want you to tell me the truth."

"Doc, I swear—"

"Then send him in tomorrow."

"It's a girl. . . . Hello, Doc? Hello!"

"A friend of yours?"

"Yeah. . . ."

"You better come in too."

"You don't understand. . . . I'm okay."

"Go home. Your mother is out of her mind. Do you hear?"

"I hear you, but I can't right now."

"Listen, Mel, don't ask me favors if you're going to act that way."

"Can she see you now?" I asked.

"She'll have to come to the office. I'll be there at nine tomorrow morning."

"She doesn't have any money."

"I'm not asking for money, I'm asking you to—"

"I tell you what I'll do, Doc. I'll call the folks tomorrow morning too."

"Tonight. How can you let them suffer?"

I thought about it. I knew they'd be upset, but suffering? That's a big thing. I knew what he meant. It's what I went through when I used to follow Vincy around and when Franklin broke off. Besides, to call them wasn't going to tie me down. At least they'd know I was alive and okay.

"Okay, Doc. I tell you what I'll do. I'll call them now and you'll take care of my friend. A deal?"

"What's her name?"

"Vincy."

"Vincy what?"

"Vincy de Havilland."

She whispered, "No. . . . I changed it to Garland."

I repeated it to Rosenberg and he said that he would wait a little bit and call my folks to see if I'd kept my end of the bargain.

"Tell her to be at my office nine sharp, please," he said. We hung up.

I was swimming in sweat and I told Vincy it was okay and gave her the address. She kissed me on the forehead and said that I could stay with her that night again.

"Can't. . . . I've got to be with Franklin. I found him and he's in trouble."

"The bastard deserves whatever it is," she said.

I didn't like that but I didn't say anything.

Then she smiled that old terrific smile. "Okay, he deserves it. But right now I'm willin' to forgive the whole friggin' world. Now, go call your folks."

Calling was a big mess but I lived through it. First thing was when Mom answered the phone, which I didn't care for. We went through the same crap about where was I? was I okay? why did I leave camp? why wasn't I home? and did I know that I'd made my father sick, he had a splitting headache and didn't sleep all last night?

I didn't like her pulling the stuff about Pop, using him to make me feel worse than I did. I tried to explain that I had to see Franklin and that there was nothing wrong with me and I was sorry I had to lie to get out of camp but that was because if I told them the truth they'd raise hell and I thought it was better my way and as soon as I could I'd go back to camp and not to worry.

That was water off a duck's back. She didn't hear a word I said but ordered me to come right home and if I didn't she didn't know what she would do with herself, and I said I couldn't and I wouldn't. Then Pop got on the phone and told me how much Mom was suffering. She also hadn't slept any and he was sure that I thought I was doing the right thing but it couldn't be if it hurt parents so much and he would try to understand if I would take the next train out of Penn Station and he'd meet me at Beachport and have a good talk and if I could convince him that what I had to do with Franklin was so important he would himself drive me back to wherever I was, wasn't that fair?

I told him that I thought it was very fair but I was old enough to know what I had to do, and I thanked him and said again that I was sorry I made so much trouble and that I'd be home in a couple of days, to go to sleep, and everything would be okay.

Then before I knew it Marcy came on and said I was irresponsible and I didn't care if I broke Mom's and Pop's hearts and to have a little consideration for others. I wanted to tell her where to put all that crap but I knew they were listening so I said good night, Marcy, and hung up.

I looked for Vincy but she wasn't outside the booth. I went around the corner. The other hookers said she had gotten herself a john and then was going to call it a night.

God, I hoped she'd have sense enough to go to Rosenberg in the morning.

28 I told Franklin about Vincy and the telephone calls to Rosenberg and my folks. He was smoking pot, sharing it with me; he said he didn't like my hurting my folks and I ought to go home the next day. I thought of what he did to Vincy but I didn't want to throw it up to him. I guess he wasn't remembering, what with all the trouble he was in. But then nobody can be hitting on all eight all the time.

I wished we'd gone somewhere else. My place was a grave. The smell from the garbage, the flies, the alley cats spitting and squealing on the roof, the loud talk across the areaway, and a screaming chick somewhere in the building all got to me. More than that, Franklin didn't want a light turned on and we were in the dark, he on the bed with his hands underneath his head and me on a half-broken chair next to him. I wasn't altogether easy in the dark. Never was. Not scared, but itchy, if you know what I mean. When I first came in I could see by the light in the hallway that Franklin had a .38 in his hand. He'd told me to lock the door from inside and put the other chair under the knob. Maybe because he was scared as hell I was too. But yet—I don't know how to say this—it was more than that. Not only was San Juan Joe somewhere out there—and it sure boiled the shit out of me to think of him—but there was something sad about the two of us.

He talked a lot suddenly. Mostly it was about himself, not really knowing his father and looking for his mother. He told me that one of the worst times in his life was once when he was walking with a friend. They were both around fifteen at the time. It was on Broad Street in Philly. And coming toward them was an old colored whore, lipstick all smeared, her hair falling over her face, her dress torn and dirty and half open at the boobs. His friend left Franklin and went over to talk to her. "When he came back," Franklin told me, "I said, 'What the hell ya doin' with an old street slut like that?' And my friend said, 'That was my Mama.' "

He closed his eyes. "Well, you know how I felt. I could've sunk myself right through the concrete. I didn't know how to make it up to him. I don't think in my whole life I've cried more than once or twice but I wanted to then. But he didn't say anything and I couldn't." He swatted a fly. "But you know what tore me up about that time, the more I thought of it? It was that someday I'd be walking along some street somewhere and see an old whore and it'd be my mother. Shee-it!"

He lay there for a while, sweating. I found an old newspaper in a closet, rolled it up, and worked on the flies. Now and then we'd hear someone in the hall, maybe going to the crapper, and he'd sit up slowly with the .38 and wait. When the water rattled—you could hear it all over the building—he'd grin and lay back. "Got your old silver bullet still there?" he asked.

"Got it," I said.

He lit another reefer. "I tell you what, Doc. If you ever think you've lost it, you got to pretend, make out, understand, that it ain't true. Don't you ever let yourself believe ya really lost it. Get it? Because if you do, if you think your gun is empty, you're not going to be worth the shit you'll have to eat. Get it, boy?"

I said yes and didn't ask questions. Besides, the pot was getting to me.

He talked a little about the war. It wasn't much different than the numbers game. It was all a question of odds. And it didn't have much more to it than that. "Although Mr. Hitler was a first-class bastard to your people, I was never sure what would have happened to mine if he'd won." He laughed a little. "More niggers in this world than Jews. He'd have himself a real hard time." He took a deep drag. "When ya think about it, there's no difference between livin' and war. Ya got your allies, your ammo, your little hill ya got to take from someone kinda like yourself. And all the while the big boys sit on their asses somewhere else. An' ya can't go through it without hurtin' someone an' bein' hurt. Ain't that life, though?"

Again, he wasn't talking the way he usually did, like when we were with Venturi and Katz and most other times. No, he was singing a little, like when he worked that puton with my folks, Amos and Andy style, if you know what I mean.

Another deep swing of the joint and he passed it to me. I let it go out. He didn't notice. So I put it in my pocket. He was staring at the ceiling and I could see a little of his face from the light coming from a window across the alley. It was wet but just as good-looking as ever. His eyes, the whites showing big, seemed strong, knowing where he was and what he wanted. I wasn't feeling scared anymore. No matter what or who was out there, Franklin, my Franklin, would find the right way to beat it.

I must've fallen asleep, because the next thing I knew it was growing light. Franklin's eyes were still on the ceiling, just the way I'd left them.

"Ya took a long time dreamin'," he said, grinning, his white teeth cutting the darkness that was still there. "But I

185

been plannin'." He sat up and put his shoes on, ran his hands over his naked body, touching his arms, legs, and between his legs like he was loving it all.

"The whole thing's connecked," he sang. "Ankle bone connecked to the leg bone, leg bone connecked to the thigh bone. . . . Yes, sir! They's all connecked—San Juan Joe, Venturi and Katz, and the big pushers. I mean, the cats in the back room, not the mice on the streets. No, sir! It's a big plate of milk, with lotsa big tiger cats, man, and I'd be a bigger fool than I am if I didn't know that. That milk ain't for me. Everybody gonna know that, so who's gonna piss on Franklin Gilboa's name 'cause he took hisself a powder and laid low for a bit, eh? When the Nazi bastards cornered us like they did at the Bulge, why we just crawfished under a bit until the weather cleared and the bombers made their runs down to the winning wire. So I tell ya what I'm goin' to do. I'm goin' to take me a train somewhere and you're gonna drive my car to Rahway, New Jersey. Dover Street and Main. Connie's Garage. . . . Jus' leave it where ya find a spot. . . . Outside, inside, it don't matter 'cause it's gonna be closed when ya get there. . . . Leave the keys in the dash. I owe Connie some back money. . . . Then go home, boy. Go home, take a long hot bath, clean yourself of this stinkin' room, Harlem, and the rackets. One of these days you'll be gettin' a call from me, long distance, and I'll be saying to ya, 'This is Mr. Gilboa here. That you, Doc, there?' And you'll say, 'Damn it, if it ain't old Franklin.' An' we'll make a plan to have us a glory time again. Got it, boy? You'll be hearin' from me."

"No."

"What's that mean?"

"I'm going to go with you."

"You're one crazy kid."

"Please!"

He laughed a little from the pot.

"Okay, Franklin?"

"I gotta move fast."

"I'll move just as fast."

"Fast means one, not two. Don't ya ever learn?"

He was dressed by then and turned to stare out the window at the gray wall of the building across the alley. The sun hadn't reached it yet.

"It's gettin' late. On your way, boy."

The way he said it I knew there wasn't a chance. I tried to be cool. "When'll I hear from you?" I said.

"Sooner or later."

He gave me the car keys and stood in the middle of the room, rubbing his knuckles, looking at me hard.

"Ya know, Doc, I ain't no Christer. Drugs is gonna be big business, and why shouldn't I get my snout onto the pig's tits like the others? But I got something they ain't got. Two things. First, I like people. Really like 'em. And I hate fuckin' 'em up. And second, I got me a kid. Ya know about him. . . ."

I didn't ask questions about Brian this time.

"I'll tell ya about him. . . ." He coughed a little. "He's so far gone on coke and horse he'll never live to be twenty. He's OD'd twice already. Get it, boy? Not twenty and he's your age to the year."

I kept staring at him, trying to let it all catch up to me.

He reached over and touched my shoulder. "Ya got enough bread to see ya home from Rahway?"

"Yeah. . . ."

Suddenly he shifted his body like a pitcher getting ready to wind up. "You'll be okay," he said. "You'll be damned okay. College and law school, hear?"

"Sure, I'll be okay."

"You know, when we first met I figured I'd teach ya how

to fuck." He laughed. "I'll be damned if I didn't teach ya what I shoulda learned myself—how to love."

What I wanted to do at that minute I couldn't do. Hell, I never remember kissing Pop.

"Better beat it now. Time's got to be on my side. That is if it ain't passed me by already. . . ."

I went to the door.

"Drive that car carefully, y'hear?"

"I will. . . ."

"Good luck, son."

I closed the door without making any noise and ran down the stairs.

29 I decided first to head downtown to the Holland Tunnel, Jersey City, and Newark. But after I'd gone a couple of blocks I got a good idea. If they'd be looking for Franklin's white Caddie while he went off wherever he was going, why not take it up to Harlem first? Someone would see it, follow me, think I was going to pick Franklin up, and in that way I'd give him more time. So I went up Fifth Avenue again and drove to 145th, up and down Lenox and Seventh. I stopped for a coke at a Rexall and looked for Vincy, but none of the hookers were up that early. I fooled around until about twelve, one o'clock. I thought that a big Lincoln was shadowing me, but when I got to the tunnel I didn't see it anymore.

Connie's Garage was open when I got there. Nobody asked any questions. I parked the Caddie, left the keys, and walked out. By three I was in New York at Penn Station. I called Dr. Rosenberg's office. He wasn't there, but the nurse said there'd been no Miss Garland in that morning. I was sore as hell and I wondered whether I ought to head uptown to find her again, but if you want to know the truth I was too bushed. The thing with Franklin had kind of scooped me out. Besides, my legs were killing me. I stopped off at a drugstore to get a malted chocolate and some more aspirin. An hour or so later, trying not to think of Franklin, I was limping up Prosser Street to my house. It was around six and the folks would be home, which was okay with me, because I thought I might as well get it all over quickly.

Prosser Street, full of kids, mostly Jewish, playing long handball from sewer cover to sewer cover, looked to me like I'd been away ten years. There was a smell of cooking I remembered, greasylike, but not the same kind of greasy smell of Harlem. Sort of like comparing week-old chicken soup with greens cooking up right then and there. The folks on Prosser sitting on their camp chairs in front of the buildings to get a little fresh air were okay; but when they laughed or yelled to the kids to be careful of traffic or to come in for supper, it was nothing like the crazy sounds of 135th Street or 116th or anywhere in Harlem from 110th to 155th, from ritzy Sugar Hill to the East River. If you listened on the radio to the schmaltz of Ben Marden's Riviera Club and then to Count Basie at Small's Paradise, you'd know what I mean. I guess the only thing I was sure of as I took that long last mile to 34 Prosser—where, God help me, Mom, Pop, and Marcy would be waiting with their little white teeth and their white angry faces and their goddamn white responsibility crap—was that niggers, as Franklin said once, may be stuck in the assholes of the world, but they're a livin', lovin' people, and I'd rather be Jackie Robinson than Joe DiMaggio any time, though they're both great baseball players.

Well, what can I tell you that you don't know already?

189

Mom and Marcy were there—Pop was still at the track, where he had gone, I was sure, to escape my problem, which I didn't blame him for—and I was pounded over the head with questions and speeches and how could I do such terrible things to my family? It got so that I yelled to them to lay off, and, forgetting everything, I said that my legs hurt so much I had to go to bed.

I fell asleep fast like I didn't ever want to think again about anything. When I woke up, old Doc Rosenberg was there with his little gray pointed beard and thick glasses.

"She didn't come, did she?"

He said no and asked questions about my legs and where the pain was and how long I'd had it. He ran his fingers up and down, pressing here and there, taking my temperature and looking down my throat. When he was finished, he turned to Mom, who had come in to watch. "I'm sure," he said, "it's not infantile paralysis. But it may be Osgood Shlatterers."

It's a helluva funny name for growing pains, but it wasn't funny when he said I'd have to have a leg splint and stay in bed for at least two weeks with hot water bottles (try that in July). Then he might decide if I could go out and sit in the sun for another couple of weeks. In the meantime he'd send a bone doctor to take a look. There was some talk of X-rays, a cast, Ace bandages, and stuff for the pain, and the only thing good about Osgood Shlatterers was that I didn't have to go back to the "Admiral's" camp and that the folks and Marcy began to treat me like I was grown-up, though with their asking me every hour on the hour how I was feeling they overdid it.

That summer wasn't much fun. I listened every day and all day to baseball and all the other shows, my favorites being Jack Benny and Fibber McGee and Molly. The political stuff between Dewey and Truman was a bomb. Mom would leave me some sandwiches, milk, and fruit for lunch and go out to make speeches for Truman or hang around Democratic headquarters. She was always hot for things like that. Now and then Pop would drive me to the Sound or a movie, trying to get me to talk about Franklin or what I wanted to do when I graduated that next June. He pitched college to me, but I told him I'd wait and see.

Franklin had taught me more than three years of Beachport High. Not that I'd figured on going into policy or horsebook. But there were lots of other things, and if you kept that silver bullet in your gun, you could ride high forever. Not forgetting Franklin being there to share the loot, the lovin', and the larkin' around.

But getting back to Pop, I was feeling sad about him. You know, living in the house like he was a paid boarder. And I thought I understood that somewhere in the old days he'd faced the fact that Mom was top dog and wouldn't be happy unless she was, so he decided to let her run. He sure must've loved her.

The truth is I didn't want to go to games or movies in case Franklin made that call he promised me. Every time the phone rang I'd yell, "Is it for me?" But it never was.

30 In September school started. Eddie Norris filled out his college application but I never brought my papers home. I was in Mr. Clothier's senior class, this time American lit, and I had to read about Huck Finn and Nigger Jim, and I liked them a helluva lot.

One day I got a picture postcard from St. Louis. It said,

"The Yanks will win this year!" It was signed Emperor Jones. Well, you don't have to be told I was riding high for a week after. Then toward the end of the month I came in from school and went into my room with a copy of the *Racing Form* to try a little handicapping. I saw *The New York Times* on my bed. Mom was always trying to get me interested in reading the *Times* rather than the *Daily News*. But this was the first time she'd put one on my bed. I turned to the sports, read Daley's column and the race results, then went back to the news just to look through it and prove to her at supper that there wasn't anything in it that the *Daily News* didn't have. Then I saw something that Mom had circled with a red crayon.

HOTEL MYSTERY GAMBLER IDENTIFIED
St. Louis (AP)—Fingerprints of a man found by a cleaning woman in the Forrest Hotel were identified by the New York police as those of Franklin Gilboa. He had been shot twice. Robbery was evidently not the motive, since money and a wristwatch were found on him. Police are looking for clues leading to the murderer.

I kept reading and reading, not thinking, not moving, not believing. Then I found myself at the dining room phone calling Em. She said it was true. She'd gotten the word and had taken care of getting Franklin back to Harlem. He was in the Foster and Smith Funeral Home and the services would be the next day. She'd have called me, she said, if she'd known where I was.

I wrote a note to the folks, ran to the Beachport station, rode through all the old towns without seeing them, ran from Penn Station to the shuttle, and took an A train up to 145th Street. I got there without knowing what I was doing half the time.

Hayes was at the funeral parlor. Em told him I was coming and he waited for me. We didn't say anything while we shook hands. I said I wanted to see Franklin alone. He talked to some people and they let me into the room.

He was dressed in a black suit and lay on a white silk bed inside the coffin. I hated to see the lipstick and the tan powder on his face. He looked like an actor, and I reached in to wipe some of the powder away. His hands were clasped together over his chest and the two broken thumbs stuck out the way I remembered. They were more Franklin to me than his face. I touched them. I could've sworn they were warm but I knew they weren't. The gold wristwatch with the diamonds and rubies was gone but it didn't make any difference with no scratch sheet to check on. Next to the wall was a big bunch of roses from the American Legion Post; there were some other flowers but they didn't have any names on them. I wondered what I had to give. What could I leave him? What could he take along? I stuck my hands in my coat pocket. I found a half-smoked joint. It was the one Franklin and I'd had our last night together. Why not smoke it right then and there? I thought. It would be only right. I tried my other pockets and found a movie stub and a page torn out of the *Racing Form*. I knew then what I'd do. I looked around. I was still alone. I leaned over the coffin and carefully put the joint and the torn page in the side pocket of Franklin's coat.

I stood there a long time thinking of everything and nothing. I didn't know Hayes had come in until he touched me.

Mom and Pop said they wanted to go to the funeral and they asked if it was okay with me so I let them. It was in the funeral parlor's Chapel of Repose, which had two stained glass windows and a phony-looking painting of Jesus. We arrived a little late because of traffic, but the service hadn't started yet. Just the organ playing. I was surprised that there weren't more people there. Hayes and Hobie, John Hemingway, wearing a black eye patch instead of the silver one, some people from Small's, Obie's, and the Cotton Club, Solly the barber, the fat old lady who worked at Hayes' spot, Chris Johnson, who owned the poker van, a couple of runners I'd met, and some customers from my territory who I had visited to break the news. Mom recognized Nat King Cole and his daughter. She was always great at recognizing famous people. Em came in, dressed in white, followed by four chicks from her place. I recognized two but they didn't smile when they saw me. The organ kept playing until the preacher entered through a side door, followed by a woman in black and a tall thin fellow my age. I figured they were Franklin's wife and Brian, but I couldn't see their faces when they sat down in the front row. I turned around to look for Vincy but she wasn't there.

When the organ stopped I could hear a couple of women sobbing. The preacher, a short man with a deep voice, read from the Bible in a kind of singsong way and then began a speech about how he didn't know the deceased well, only by reputation, but could tell by the look of the folks who had come to pay their last respects that he must've been a good man, loved and respected by all, an honorable citizen, a family man whose wife and son had a great weight of sorrow to carry. And so on and so on. I didn't follow him all the way. I was thinking of the reefer and *Racing Form* in Franklin's pocket. They were more him than all the jerk stuff the preacher spilled.

The organ played again and the preacher asked the family and pallbearers to come forward. The woman and Brian walked past the coffin without stopping and left through a side door.

194

In the street a big crowd of neighborhood people gathered around the door. Someone yelled, "There's Nat King Cole," and kids ran over for autographs. A car parked behind the hearse began to move out. Venturi and Katz were in it. My legs and arms started shaking and I wanted to yell, "Stop them! They killed Franklin!" But they were away before I could hear the words in my head. Pop must've noticed something wrong. He put his hand on my arm and asked if I was okay. I nodded and took some deep breaths to keep from passing out.

The coffin was carried out of the chapel by Hayes, Hobie, John Hemingway, and Solly the barber. Behind them were Brian and his mother, who was not bad-looking but kind of flat. The kid took after Franklin, the same color and the eyes. But there was no dance in his face. He looked like he had just gotten up from sleep and he stumbled and grabbed his mother's arm. She said something and he looked at his watch. It was Franklin's. I hated to see it on him, then I thought: What the hell? He never had half of what I had.

Hayes' fat old dame ran up to put a flower on the coffin and yelled, "Good-bye, honey! Ya goin' to heaven! Sweet man goin' to heaven!" She kept yelling until they shoved the coffin into the hearse and closed the doors with a loud click of the latch.

Mom said she didn't think it was a good idea to go to the grave. Pop didn't say anything as usual, and I didn't argue. Who wants to see his best friend in the world shoveled over with dirt? What I lost wasn't going to be given back in any cemetery.

31 I stayed in bed—I don't remember how long—dreaming no dreams, sleeping dead, not eating, not talking, not listening to the radio, hands and legs like they were cut off, nothing left to move, not wanting to move. I heard sounds inside my head that I didn't want to hear, saw pictures of him in the coffin that I didn't want to see. Man, I was full of grief. . . .

There was nothing in the papers about who killed him. I thought I ought to tell the cops about Venturi and Katz, but what would that do? What cop would believe me? What cop wasn't on the take?

Mom and Marcy tried to make me feel better, saying they were sorry too. Pop didn't say much but sat next to the bed, fixing the blankets when I dozed off or turned. Once he brought up the World Series, but he saw I didn't care so he dropped it. Marie Anderhorst, Diana Levy, and my Uncle Jack came by. I was a hero to them because I knew a guy who was murdered. . . .

One night Eddie Norris came over to bull around but I couldn't take it anymore. I had to do something. Franklin couldn't die just like that! I had called Em maybe for the tenth time, but she had no news and wasn't expecting any. She told me that some new people had taken over Franklin's policy territory, Harlem was beginning to stink bad with the pushers, and there was talk in the streets about a preacher from Chicago who was starting a new religion to fight drugs, a Mr. Elijah Muhammad, and she might go uptown soon to hear him.

I didn't want any new religion. I wanted to fight back. To

kill the killers. To do anything. I told Eddie I was going to the beach. He said he'd go along. I didn't want him to and I said so. That hurt his feelings but the hell with it. I was hurting all over.

I bought a pint of Four Roses from a new guy at Kaplan's Liquor and Deli who took the dough, saying, "You're a minor, ain't ya? It's for your old man, ain't it?" He wouldn't have cared if I'd have said, "Yeah, the old man in the moon." I stuck the pint in my belt under my white jacket and limped over to the beach. The wind was socking the waves until they broke against the beach like a waterfall. I like it when it's rough on a clear night with the moon and everything. I found a good place under the boardwalk—not many people were around—and with my hands I dug a long hole big enough to lie in. Sand was blowing up but not too much. Anyway, I opened the pint, took a couple of slugs, and covered my head with the jacket.

I wanted to get drunk and fall asleep and maybe let the sand bury me. The wind and ocean were getting louder, and I took a couple of more slugs and fixed the jacket around my head, tying the arms together. After a while I fell asleep. And I had this dream. I was at a funeral but I didn't know who was dead. There was a hell of a crowd in the place. I didn't recognize anybody. And nobody seemed to know me. The queer thing was everybody, I mean, everybody, was colored in a kind of silver light or else was wearing silver clothing. The whole place was silver. I didn't know if it was a church or a synagogue or Siegel's Memorial Parlor, when one of my aunts died.

In my dream I tried to push my way through the crowd to where the coffin was. "Let me through! Let me through!" I yelled, but the only thing coming out of my mouth was silver-colored bubble gum, which broke all over my face. The more I yelled, the more bubbles came pouring out, until my mouth was filled with them. I was drowning in the silver shit.

Nobody paid any attention to me and that scared me more than anything. I prayed to God. Which is funny because I didn't believe in God, and even if I did, why the hell should He pay any attention to Doc Henshel?

I yelled, "Hey, it's Doc! It's Doc!" But the only thing that came out was the bubble gum.

Suddenly everybody disappeared. I was alone. At the far end of the room lay the large silver coffin. In it was Franklin, stiff and queer, silvered like the rest. His hands were clasped over his chest with the two broken thumbs sticking out. I felt terrible.

"Hey, you! Walyo! Get up outta there!"

Something kept hitting my legs. I opened my eyes. My face was covered with my jacket and I couldn't see anything.

I pushed the jacket away. A cop was tapping his night stick against my legs. The moon behind silvered him like the others and I thought I was still dreaming. His flashlight passed over my face.

"You drunken punk, get the hell up here!"

It wasn't the dream anymore. I was dizzy when I stood up and, what's more, scared shitless. He was a big guy with a watermelon belly. He picked up the Four Roses and asked me my name, address and how old I was. I couldn't think fast enough so I told him the truth.

He said he was going to book me for making a public nuisance and then take me home to watch my father wallop the hell out of me.

Franklin told me something once about how to handle cops, but what? I moved as slowly as I could, trying to remember, shaking the sand off my jacket and pants.

Then it came to me. Cops are the greatest slobs in the world. They'll cry over a sick cat as quick as they'll throw a night stick at a guy lifting a ten-cent loaf of bread. Try to get 'em in the slob department, he said.

"I had a good reason to drink a little tonight," I said. "I was sad. My best friend died."

It wasn't getting to him. Not a wrinkle on his face moved. I figured if I told him about Franklin it wouldn't mean a thing. So I said, "My family. . . ."

"Yeah. . . ."

By this time he had marched me from under the board-walk toward the steps.

"My Aunt Rose," I said. "My favorite aunt. . . ."

"When she die?"

That was real encouraging and I made a full report that she died yesterday in the Bronx, had been a WAAC in the war, worked for General Eisenhower, a real patriotic American woman who was more like a mother than an aunt and I was real tore up about it.

"Everybody's got an Aunt Rose," he said. It didn't sound good.

I tried to see if he was Irish, Italian, or Jewish. I was ready to go any way. His eyes were close together, his nose turned up a little, and he had a long jaw. Not a clue. Eddie Norris' father looked more like a mick than Bing Crosby. You can never tell. . . .

"She was half Irish," I said. "And half Italian." Even if he was Jewish, I thought, that would help, because the Jews I know sometimes make a big play for the other kind. "And she was young too. No more than thirty maybe. And pretty. Boy, was she pretty."

"That's young," he said, and I thought I had him.

"And she taught Sunday School too."

"Where?"

Damn it, I never know when to stop talking. I had to get out of that stupid remark fast. "I don't know exactly. In the

Bronx somewhere. Saint Something." I looked up at him as if he was a holy priest.

"And ya want me to let ya go because ya heart was breakin', is that it?"

I didn't have to answer that.

"Ya know it's against the law drinkin' on the beach?"

"Yes, sir."

"But ya did it anyway."

"I couldn't help myself, officer."

He looked at the bottle. There was still a lot left in it. "Okay." He took a deep breath, then belched and poured the whisky on the sand. "You just tell me where you bought this crap and I'll let ya go."

Wow! The bastard had me, because I wasn't going to snitch even on that dopey clerk at Kaplan's. Franklin wouldn't like it, and I felt rotten even thinking about it.

"Well, how about it, sonny?"

He sounded like an old buddy, the louse.

"Gee, officer, I can't do that."

"Do what, Mel?"

"I can't tell you."

"Why not?"

"I can't." I was sweating and it wasn't the heat.

"Well, that's up to you."

"But it'll only be worse, sir."

"What could be worse, punk?"

What if I told him I'd swiped it from Pop? He'd take me home and I'd be a goner. I was stumped. I mean, what do you do in a case like that? If you don't tell the truth you're in the soup; if you do you're a shit. If he could only have been satisfied with my name, rank, and serial number like they do in the movies.

"How about it, kid?" The cop was getting pushy.

The wind and ocean had died down a little and I felt I was

alone in the whole world in the middle of nowhere with no light, no air, no place to go—and no Franklin anymore. I thought: Shit, why not tell him? So he'll go to Kaplan and get the clerk fired; he was a jerk anyway to sell the stuff to a minor. Or else the cop'd work old Kaplan for a couple of extra bucks a week to keep him from getting a summons. What the hell did I really care for the clerk or Kaplan? But, man oh man, if Franklin could get his thumbs broke, why couldn't I take a chance on getting booked for drinking in a public place? So Pop and Mom would raise hell and I'd have a police record.

There had to be a way out, but all I could think of saying was "I can't tell."

The cop nipped my arm and walked me up the steps to the boardwalk.

We were near the Sunset Arcade. I pulled away and he grabbed me.

"Don't try a funny on me," he said.

"Okay, officer, I'll tell you the truth."

He waited.

Well, there are truths and there are truths, as Franklin used to say. Legit crimes and illegit crimes. "I stole the whisky," I said, feeling like Joan of Arc and Nathan Hale.

He let go of my arm. "Yeah, that's what I thought. From who?"

"Kaplan's Liquor. . . ."

"Okay, kid, I'm glad you told me the truth. Ya should've done it right away. It always saves a lot of trouble. I'm not goin' to run ya in this time. But you'll go with me right now to Kaplan's. You'll tell him and make it up to him by workin' or payin' for it."

He walked me back to the store. Kaplan wasn't there, only the dopey clerk, who was scared right out of his pants. But he wasn't that dopey that he didn't put on a big act and say he'd seen me in there looking over the comic mags and when his back was turned I must have pinched the Four Roses from the counter.

"Next time, kid," he said in a nasty sour-milk voice, "ya won't be robbin' Mr. Kaplan."

The cop said, "How much was it?"

It was under two bucks and I gave him a five.

"Keep the change," the cop said. "It'll teach him a lesson."

"Thank you, officer," the louse said, then turned to me. "That'll teach ya to keep your dirty hands off other people's property."

"Shut up!" I said.

"Up yours!"

I was ready to break the guy into splinters but the cop told me to knock it off. "If ya don't learn now, you'll never learn."

Well, I sure learned. You want to make it, tell lies that sound like truths and truths that sound like lies. And I thought how I'd never be able to tell that to Franklin and I was ready to bawl but I wouldn't give them the satisfaction.

32 Pop was out somewhere calling on an insurance prospect, and Mom was collecting money for Israel or distributing stuff for Truman. I went over to Solomon's Arms, on the corner of Mulvey and Webster, where Franklin used to live when he ran the Sunset Arcade. The super was a mick who always had a bad cold, but I thought he was on the booze. At least he smelled that way. I asked if I could see Franklin's old room.

"He's been out of it a year," he said. "What ya want to see it for?"

"Just to see it."

"Nothin' in it. Some colored kid about your age came by and took the stuff away. Had a court order. Gave me a tip too."

"That's okay. I don't want anything."

"Why ya want to go in if there's nothin' there?"

Christ, what could I say if I didn't know myself? "Look, mister, can I go in or not?"

He coughed, spit into a garbage can, wiped his nose with a rag, and said, "Don't get feisty with me, bub."

I gave him a buck and he said, "If ya want to, go ahead."

The locks had been taken off and I walked right inside. The lights weren't working. It was dark except for some yellow spill coming through a high cellar window. All the chick pictures had been taken down and torn up. Pieces lay all over the floor near the wall. The bed wasn't there, just the springs. And there was the old broken-down blue velvet easy chair. I looked around. I thought I could still smell some maryjane but I wasn't sure.

Mice scuttled across the floor. I turned at the sound and walked to the wall and ran my fingers across it where the chick pictures used to hang. Then along the bookcases where some old copies of the *Racing Form* were still piled up. I took one, wiped the dust off, folded it, and stuck it in my back pocket. I went back to sit in the chair and looked up at the pipes on the ceiling. They were sweating.

Franklin'd reach over from the chair to the Emerson and turn on some jazz. That's where he'd play the records for me. I guessed Brian had taken it with all the good platters. I leaned back and closed my eyes. . . .

I remembered how I told him to get fifty-one percent from Hayes and Hobie.

What ya want to do when you grow up?

I touched the table without looking.

Legit and legit. . . . Odds. . . . Ain't worth a crap on a sheet of pink toilet paper. . . .

The mice made a helluva racket in the torn pictures, little devils, going like crazy looking for something.

Goin' to college?

Christ, I was so sure I heard him I looked around behind me. The door of the can was open. I saw a couple of broken records on the floor. I went over. One of them was Basie's "Slow Boat to China." I felt like kicking that Brian where he'd remember too.

I went to college. . . .

I turned back to the chair. I could've sworn he was there.

"Oh, Franklin! . . . Oh, Franklin!"

I stood next to the empty chair, leaned on the blue velvet, and cried like a goddamn baby.

33 The next day, Saturday, I got up before anyone else, made some orange juice and a peanut butter sandwich, and went back into my bedroom to eat breakfast by myself. The bathroom door was open—Marcy was staying with some of her college friends for the weekend. I didn't know what to do with myself. There wasn't anybody in the world but me. I could hear the creaking of the walls and floors and someone in the street slamming a door. I remembered the dream when suddenly everybody disappeared and I was alone with Franklin in his coffin all silvered up. I thought of Eddie Norris going off to college, knowing what he wanted to do with his life. All I wanted was not to be seventeen, not to have to decide anything, or maybe jump ten years and be all grown up with everything done. I thought of Franklin's mother. How he never met her again. . . . That was a part of him no one knew, except maybe Em. But, I guess, we all have these lost people in our lives. . . .

The door opened. Pop stood there in his pajama pants. His skinny white chest and arms made him seem very old. We said good morning to each other and he sat down on the bed.

"From the looks of it," he said, "you make a neat peanut butter sandwich."

"Want a piece?" I hadn't touched it.

He nodded and tore it in half. He chewed it and then said it made him thirsty. I gave him the glass of orange juice.

"What're you going to do today?"

"I don't know. . . ."

"How about going to the races with me?"

He hadn't asked me for a long time. Maybe when I was seeing Franklin he didn't want to be shown up alongside a real pro. I wasn't sure of any of this but I saw the look in his eyes when he said, "Why not, Mel? It would be good to get out—together?" I thought: Damn it, he looks and sounds alone, like me. I never figured that parents had the same problems as their kids. I thought of Mom and how she ran him and the family. I guessed he must have his own days of getting up early and making breakfast to be by himself. And, who knows, running off to the races to be alone in that great noisy crowd.

But today he wanted me to go with him. I watched as he chewed the peanut butter and washed it down with the juice. Christ, he needed me and that was okay.

I took the empty plate and glass. "Want some more, Pop?"

He smiled. "I ate your breakfast."

"So what? We can have us a bite at the races."

He bent over and kissed the top of my head.

34 One day when I was home alone the telephone rang and when I answered a man asked for Mr. Henshel. I said he wasn't home, could he leave a message? The man said to have him call Mr. Venturi and he gave me the telephone number. I asked which Mr. Henshel did he want? There was no sound on the phone for a moment, then the voice said, "The young Mr. Henshel."

"That's me," I said.

The man said, "Hold on."

Venturi came to the phone. "You the fellow who's a friend of Franklin's?" he asked.

"Yeah. . . ." I wanted to hang up and spit.

"I got something important to tell you. Come to my office. You were here once."

"What for?"

"It's in your interest."

"Tell me what for."

"Not on the phone."

"The hell with it then!"

"Look, young man," Venturi said. "I'm not calling you to hear myself talk. You going to come in or aren't you? What we got to say is to your benefit. Get here tomorrow afternoon between four and five." He hung up.

I didn't know what to do or who to ask for advice. If they were behind Franklin's murder, maybe they wanted to do the same to me because I was there with him when they threatened him. I played with that idea for a while and then I figured that if they wanted to kill me they wouldn't ask me to come to the office. They could pick me up in Beachport any time they wanted. That idea, which made sense, didn't make me feel any better. I was scared either way. Then I remembered Franklin and Till, and Franklin giving Till back his gun. But I had to play it smart.

I went out and whistled up to Eddie Norris' window and yelled to him to come down. We took a walk on the beach and I said not to ask me any questions but would he go to New York with me tomorrow while I saw someone connected with Franklin?

"All I want you to do is hang around outside the office until I come out, okay?"

Eddie knew how I felt about Franklin's death and he was willing to go along if I'd explain in advance what it was all about.

"I can't," I said.

"Then why should I go?"

"Because I need you. Because we're friends."

He kicked up some sand. "You never needed me before, except to do your homework with you."

"This is different."

"What's different?"

"Christ, Eddie, it's different, that's all."

"When Franklin was alive, you didn't know I existed. That night you pretended you were sick at the arcade, you remember? I waited for you outside and you just walked off with him. And when we lied to your folks and went to New York together, you ditched me and went with him. Never once did you let me meet him. You were Mr. Big Shot and I was only good enough to help you with exams."

"I'm sorry, Eddie. I didn't know you felt that way. Why didn't you say so?"

"I tried to but you weren't listening."

I told him I was listening now and that things weren't the same. This time I had to do something and I didn't want to do it alone. I needed a friend, and if he came along I'd swear that if he ever needed me for anything, anything at all, for the rest of our lives, he could count on me.

"I swear to God," I said. "I swear on my Pop's life."

I think he saw that I meant it, and he suddenly smiled. "Hell," he said, "when we were kids together in the Arrow AC, we swore then to be friends forever. Okay. . . . When do we go?"

I put out my hand and he took it, fumbling around with his fingers. "I'm trying to remember the old secret grip," he said.

I didn't remember either and I thought it was one thing I'd never forget.

I told him to wait on the street in front of 500 Fifth Avenue. "If I'm not down in an hour, you call a cop and go up to the offices of Venturi and Katz. Okay?"

He was hopping from one foot to another, scared and excited, but all he did was nod and we checked our watches.

There was a girl at the desk and I told her I had an appointment with Mr. Venturi. She said to go right in. I walked through the swinging gate, remembering the last time I was there, and I told myself not to think of that time but to keep cool as hell.

I knocked on the door and Venturi called to me to come in. He was alone, sitting at his desk. Katz wasn't there and I was glad of that.

"Can I get you a coke?" Venturi asked.

"No."

"You did a smart thing coming," he said. "Sit down."

I didn't move.

"You in a hurry?"

"Yeah."

"Okay, I like people who want to get to the point." He picked up a pencil and rolled it in his fingers. "I saw you at the funeral. It was sad for all of us. I liked Franklin. I respected him."

I kept my eyes on his.

"I asked around. You were a close friend of Franklin's, weren't you? . . . Okay, I know all about you and him, how you used to run for him and even what plans he had for the two of you." He put the pencil down. "You know Hobie, don't you?"

I nodded.

"He's working for a client of mine now." He got up from the desk and walked around to stand behind a chair.

"You know I had an interest in Franklin's business. He owed me a lot of money and friends of mine took it over. There was some trouble with his son but we gave him a piece. And now we want to give you a piece."

"Why?"

"Because you're a smart kid from everything I heard."

"You want to give me a piece of what?"

"What do you want? The bowling alley, Em's, policy?"

I felt a little shaky all of a sudden. For a moment I thought of Harlem and being on my own, living the way Franklin lived, free and easy. Then I thought of Franklin saying once that his life was a little hard cash and lots of trembling and that he wanted me to go legit—not to die the way he did in a dirty room in St. Louis. And this was the man who had ordered his death.

"You trying to bribe me?" I said.

Venturi's eyes closed like a camera shutter and he clenched his fingers together in two fists. "Where the fuck did you get that idea?"

"You set up Franklin."

"Kid, you're crazy."

"You want me in the rackets to get a hold on me."

"You've seen too many movies, kid."

"You and Katz had him killed."

Venturi undid the fists, took a long breath, and moved back to his desk. He sat down and opened a drawer. I was ready to run but he reached in and his hand came out with a cigar.

"If you got evidence, why don't you go to the police or the DA?"

I didn't say anything and watched while he clipped the cigar butt, lit it, and blew out a long trail of smoke.

"That's a terrible thing you said, kid."

I stared at him.

"It could make trouble for you."

What did Franklin say to Till? I'm not going to spend the rest of my life scared.

"Mr. Venturi," I said, trying to keep my voice from trembling and holding my hands tight against my legs, "maybe some day I'm going to make trouble for you." Then, not hearing myself, I said, "So you'll know that you can't knock me off the way you did Franklin, I've written down everything that happened in this office that day."

Then like a damn fool I turned around, my back to the desk where he sat, and walked to the door like it was the last mile.

Going down the elevator, I was still trembling and ready to puke. Even when I saw Eddie pacing up and down in front of the building like a Marine on duty, I didn't feel any better.

"Okay?" he said, and he seemed real glad to see me.

"I need a cup of java," I said, and we went toward Madison to the nearest coffee shop.

I didn't know I had burned my tongue on the hot coffee until later.

Eddie was great and asked no questions, which was okay with me because I couldn't really remember a word of what had happened. All I knew was that I was Franklin's boy, but legit in a legit world in maybe five, seven years. The A train could go both ways. . . .

When we got off at the Beachport station, I put my arm around Eddie and said I'd never forget him, like I promised, and he said, "A funny thing, Doc. When I was waiting for you, I remembered the grip. It goes like this."

He linked his fingers in mine and we shook hands.